THE GUNMAN
AND THE ACTRESS

To be paid a heap of money just for protecting a fancy French actress and her troupe of players whilst they visited the wild west town didn't seem that difficult. But Joshua Dillard hadn't banked on the charms of the actress, and the fact that someone did not want him even to reach the town. And how come Bennett Maxwell wasn't as friendly as one would expect for an employer? All would be revealed in a wild chase and a blazing showdown . . .

Books by Chap O'Keefe
in the Linford Western Library:

GUNSMOKE NIGHT

CHAP O'KEEFE

THE GUNMAN AND THE ACTRESS

Complete and Unabridged

LINFORD
Leicester

First published in Great Britain in 1995 by
Robert Hale Limited
London

First Linford Edition
published 1997
by arrangement with
Robert Hale Limited
London

British Library CIP Data

O'Keefe, Chap
   The gunman and the actress.—Large print ed.—
Linford western library
   1. English fiction—20th century
   2. Large type books
   I. Title
   823.9′14 [F]

                                 LP

   ISBN 0–7089–5049–3

Published by
F. A. Thorpe (Publishing) Ltd.
Anstey, Leicestershire

Set by Words & Graphics Ltd.
Anstey, Leicestershire
Printed and bound in Great Britain by
T. J. Press (Padstow) Ltd., Padstow, Cornwall

This book is printed on acid-free paper

1

Borderland Bandits

THE raw liquor pushed to Joshua Dillard across the slop-stained *cantina* counter in the last squalid township in Mexican territory bore no resemblance to the fine product proclaimed on the bottle's label.

He was hot and trail-weary and popskull whiskey he could do without. His temper snapped.

"What moonshine is this cougar's piss?" he spluttered.

"Cougar's peess, *señor*? I theenk not," he was told in contradiction of his tortured gullet's evidence. "*Muy bueno.* Eet ees sheeped from the United States of Amereeca an' cost mooch *dinero!*"

"You're a double-damned greaser liar!" Joshua knew a racket when he saw one. He'd lost enough to crooks in

1

his lifetime. Big things. Consequently, there was nothing like being made the victim of even small-time thievery to get his dander up.

He picked up a heavy brass cuspidor and heaved it at his host's head, dispatching him to dreamland.

Bedlam broke out, with Joshua luckily not its sole focus. The motley patrons of *la raza cosmica* decided an untended bar meant all drinks were on the house. They rapidly primed themselves with tequila and mescal.

Fists swung and bottles flew.

But old Mexico was not the place for a solitary gringo to get stroppy. And besides, Joshua had had a bellyful of the enervating Mexican climate and the wind and the sand. He was already heading someplace else where he had paying business. To Argos City, two or three hours north of the Border. The job sounded kind of grand and interesting to boot . . .

A celebrated French actress on tour was about to play the local opera house, and ex-Pinkerton Dillard was hired to join up with her troupe there, to advise on her safety and protection as she progressed triumphantly from cow town to mining town across the barely tamed American frontier.

That Joshua's bank balance was dwindling — again — was reason enough for him to make haste to Gisèle Bourdette's side. But the reports he'd read were tempting, too. It seemed the actress, though capricious and out of favour with the prestigious Comédie Française in her homeland, was the most beautiful and desirable woman in the world . . . Or so she herself evidently had the compulsion and the appetite to convince its populations.

Long a widower and not addicted to casual dalliance, Joshua Dillard was still a red-blooded male. The idea of holding this fabulous creature's pretty hand, while being paid for it, promised to be no bad deal.

So as general confusion and drunken disorder held sway in the *cantina*,

Joshua took judicious advantage and snuck out of the insalubrious place and its entire neck of the woods . . . before a hothead drew a gun, unsheafed a knife.

It was high time he hit the road anyhow.

★ ★ ★

Joshua had forded the broad Rio in a hurry. He'd barely paused to sling Colt Peacemaker and cartridge belt around his neck to keep them clear of the chill water.

Now, riding north across southern Texas, he had the peace and freedom of the vast open spaces. The only life in sight was a flock of buzzards wheeling high in the brassy sky. He wondered at that. Inquiry — the habit of a lifetime — narrowed his faded blue eyes. With a flick of the rein ends, he sent his horse climbing to the rim of a sandstone bluff.

Joshua was well-mounted on a willing,

range-bred black. A coat of this colour was not universally considered to indicate grit — blacks were unfavoured among men who worked with cattle, for instance — but Joshua had followed his own hunch in his choice. The black's 'bread basket' showed he could carry food for a long ride, and crossing the two hundred yards of the Rio Grande he had proven a duck-like ability in the swimming water.

Joshua laid his hand in a gentle pat upon the animal's glossy neck. "Only an hour to Argos City, I reckon, hoss."

He sat tall in the saddle on the eminence of the crumbling red bluff, the sun beating down hotly on the crown and broad brim of his Stetson and the dusty, square-set shoulders of his coat. In the scale of the huge, semi-desert landscape of greys and ochres and russets, his powerful figure was dwarfed. Nonetheless, he maintained a certain stature, had there been eyes to observe — an indefinable quality beyond the matter of size and his shabby garb.

From his vantage point, Joshua saw a bunch of cattle gathered at a waterhole. Nothing strange about that. But why the buzzards? Had one of the beasts been injured, or butchered by thieves?

He never knew himself quite why he did it, but when he rode down from the rim, instead of rejoining the meandering stage road, he picked his way through patches of brush and cacti, prickly-pear and ocotillo, toward the pasture. "Maybe I oughta push on to Argos City," he told himself. "But I just hate mysteries and I'm gonna take a look-see."

The buzzards soared and wheeled above on near motionless wings, like black ashes caught in an updraught from a burning pit. The ex-detective steered his course by them.

The bawling of cattle came to his ears; no need now for the buzzards' ominous signposting. A sloping incline formed part of the bowl around the animals' watering place. Hereabouts, coarse buffalo grass grew thickly.

There were some fifty head of them. They were long-legged, Southern cattle, pale-coloured and of Spanish ancestry. Texas Longhorns. At frequent intervals, several of the beasts would bellow fractiously and paw at the ground.

Joshua noted they all carried the same brand — B-Bar-M.

He frowned in puzzlement at their strange behaviour. Usually only the smell of blood would make them act in this cantankerous fashion, but when he drew nearer he got an inkling of the trouble. The irritable critters were red-eyed and gave off dry heat in visible shimmers. They were running a high fever, probably the infamous Texas or red water fever, fatal to less hardy breeds, but not necessarily to Longhorns.

So that explained it. He shrugged. "C'mon, hoss, we've wasted our time, I guess."

Abandoning the detour, Joshua

rejoined the stage road and proceeded north. Shortly, the trail wound past a clump of tall mesquites. The trees were dense, but really no different from any other patch of mesquite woodland in a transitional region where diverse species of vegetation were juxtaposed.

The black's ears twitched and his steps faltered. Weary himself, Joshua misread the signs of the horse's disquiet as the balkiness brought on by fatigue. He pushed with his knees.

"Guess we better get along, feller," he urged. "Ain't no use resting up when we're practically there."

Joshua was about to touch his spurred heels to the black's flanks when a gun spat viciously from the mesquites. A slug whistled close by Dillard's head and the black reared up in sudden fright.

Joshua grabbed for the worn and cracked butt of his Peacemaker. He was a professional fighter and the greased cutaway holster was tied securely to his trouser leg to ensure smoothness in drawing. The familiar iron was in his fist and spurting back lead before another shot could be fired at him. But when the next shot came from the thicket, it wasn't one but a whole five!

At this point he figured the faster he moved, the better. He was purely outnumbered by the bushwhackers, whoever they were, and it made more sense to be a moving target than a sitting duck. He pulled the black's head around and struck off at a zigzagging gallop away from the road.

His assailants emerged from cover in pursuit. "Mexes!" Joshua grunted, turning in the saddle to glimpse them.

The band rode sinewy, under-sized ponies and even without their sombreros, the sallow skins and black moustaches would have made them unmistakable. They were dressed in coarse white cotton and with the crossed bandoleers affected by Mexican *guerrillos*. Dark eyes glittered with the lust for murder.

Joshua wondered if he'd been pursued from the *cantina* in Chihuahua. But he quickly discounted that. He'd ridden too fast to have been overtaken, and even the Spanish pride that might be part of the Mestizos' heritage did not demand vengeance for what had been a bar-room brawl. More likely, these were opportunist road agents — hungry raiders from a land that had been wasted over the years by armies and governments from both sides of the Border till *ranchero* and *peon* alike were reduced to a pitiful poverty.

It was apparent they had been waiting here patiently for some time, probably watching his approaching dust banner. They had been patient, too, not using their carbines, but lying low in the thicket till they had him dead to rights, virtually eyeball to eyeball.

He did not try to get another shot off; his plan was to get out of their hand-gun range pronto. So he holstered his own weapon and adopted the old Indian trick, sliding down to lie along the black's side to dodge the wild lead they might sling at him.

Off trail, the going was rough. "We darest not go breakneck, hoss," he gritted. "Or we'll do exactly that — or bust a leg mebbe."

To be dismounted would be to be dead. Mindful of the risks, Joshua spurred the black only lightly. Impelled by the Mexicans' gunfire, the beast needed little encouragement. But the black had come a long way and was tired, while the waiting ambushers' inferior mounts had freshness on their side.

Before long, Joshua knew they were being overhauled.

Joshua slipped out his Colt again. The lie of the land suggested that northwards were more level plains where his horse could possibly outrun the Mexes' ponies. But that was guesswork and took no account of the fatigue factor. He would have to show a dissuasive hand here and now, to curtail the chase.

His pursuers were gaining on him, coming closer and closer. He heard the hammering of their hoofs right behind him now. More cracks of gunfire and a twitch at his sleeve told him the bandits were too close for comfort.

Swinging the black at right angles, he hefted his six-shooter and aimed at the leading Mex, squinting along the barrel. The conditions did not lend themselves to fancy marksmanship. If he hit the Mex or his mount anywhere, so well and good.

Joshua let the revolver's hammer fall.

The bullet thudded into the rider's chest, spilling him from the pony's back so that he tangled with its hind legs. The animal lost its footing and collapsed in a hurtling ball of dust and thrashing limbs.

Wild human and animal screams rent the air. There was consternation and pain and anger. And fear.

"That's given the sonsofbitches something to think about," Joshua approved. But he was also thinking himself, fast. The respite could not last. Though he carried a Winchester stowed in a saddle-boot, he had just two cartridges left in the cylinder of his Peacemaker, since he always kept one chamber empty to avoid accidents. Sanctuary northwards remained uncertain. Thus he preferred to gamble on what he already knew.

A desperate, rough-and-ready plan took shape in his mind.

Joshua swerved back the way he had come. The capable black called up hidden reserves of strength and fairly leaped across the arid rock and through the patches of stunted brush. The Mexicans regained control over the frightened wits of their ponies, dug in their spurs and resumed the manhunt.

Guided by the circling buzzards, Joshua ran straight for the herd of half-wild Longhorns slinking around the waterhole. The outlying bulls, acting sentinel, raised their heads, scenting him.

Under normal circumstances, and full of grass and water, the cattle would be docile, excepting maybe for protective cows with yearling calves. Stampedes were caused by hunger and thirst, and triggered by the unexpected — a flash of lightning, a clap of thunder, a harassing wild animal.

For his tactic to succeed, Joshua was counting on the edginess brought on by the sickness he had seen in these animals. Fever would have given some at least unquenchable thirst. And he thought he could provide the stimulus to get the herd running.

The tetchy bulls raised their heads. Red eyes glowered at his pell-mell approach. Then they bellowed. Joshua's hopes soared when one pawed the ground and tore up grass with its horns. Flirting with danger, he galloped closer before firing his Colt over the ailing beasts at point-blank range.

Up went the bovine heads and they made off at a thundering pace. Panic quickly infected the others and they lumbered after the leaders.

For Joshua, it was now a case of

putting the surging tide of flashing hoofs and tossing horns between self and Mexicans.

And that was exactly what he did in short order.

The Mexicans' ponies were not trained cattle-horses. Nor were the men themselves experienced or equipped as *vaqueros*, though it was from men of their race that the Texan cowboys themselves had first learned the art of herding cattle on horseback. Without the tricks of the trade, Joshua's drygulchers were forced to retreat before the bawling mass, while their quarry skedaddled down its farthest flank.

Even so, one sombreroed rider was engulfed. His terrified pony tried to turn amidst the hot, stinking bodies of the jostling beeves. A big-framed cow, all of a thousand pounds, hooked curved horns under the obstructing belly and threw pony and man bodily over her head. They fell screaming onto the backs of the following cattle.

In moments, both had vanished — crushed and trampled beneath the grinding, pounding press of heavy flesh and bone in unstoppable motion.

When the fifty head of cattle had passed by, Joshua Dillard was a small plume of dust on the horizon, putting more ground between himself and the men who had tried to stop him.

The three Mexicans still breathing did not try to follow him. Sickly-faced, they scurried away on their ponies like dogs whipped to within an inch of their lives.

Back once more on the road to Argos City, Joshua was dust-covered and running with sweat. He slackened his hard-pushed black to an easy canter. "Sure is one thing . . . them there dago highwaymen will think twice afore pulling that stunt again," he told the horse.

At this time, it had still not struck him that he might have been anything else than the random victim of robbers or Border malcontents.

16

2

The Rage of Loco Louey

LUIS VELARDE was a man with two faces. To the *peons* of the borderlands, and to his own falsely proud self, he was a courageous rebel leader, challenging the feudally-minded *rancheros* and the rich *gringos* who were seen as natural persecutors. Robin Hood under another name in another clime.

But to the Anglo society of the South-West and its peace enforcement officers, such as the Texas Rangers. Velarde was 'Loco Louey', a brutish Mexican bandit chieftain whose gang had rustled stock, robbed banks, stuck up stagecoaches and killed honest lawmen.

His hideout was in poor country off the higher back trails where few men travelled. The canyon was a fertile oasis in the barren, wind-scoured desolation. The few unfortunates who ever came upon it by chance did so suddenly, topping a rise and working around a narrow ledge with a sheer drop of close to a thousand feet. In the midst of the towering, jagged rocks was a dense stand of live oak containing a sizeable clearing where mean *adobe* hovels and foul-odoured *jacal* huts were set around a rill.

Only one structure looked sound — a long, steep-roofed, stone-walled *posada*, with hitch racks out front. This was Loco Louey's own private dwelling, from where he ruled an empire of crime that straddled the Border and took in, besides general thievery, the cultivation, manufacture and trafficking of narcotics and the 'protection' of *perdidas* — the lost ones — toiling in small-town brothels.

When Velarde's surviving trio of shot-up, shaken-up *pistoleros* reported here from the abortive mission to kill Joshua Dillard, they did not see the big, brotherly outlaw and staunch leader of faithful *compañeros*. The darker side of his nature was displayed.

They were confronted with a cruel and ruthless gang boss in a rage. As they began to tell their halting story, Velarde's swarthy face darkened and his protuberant brown eyes bulged.

"*Caramba!* What the hell has happened? Where are Miguel and Gustavo?" He flung a half-smoked marijuana cigarette into the wide fireplace. Though he was a large man, with a *poncho* straining his black silk shirt and gold-braided gaucho jacket vest, the desperado came out of his chair in one cat-like motion. The smoke-scented air seemed to explode with his curse.

Alfonso Mendoza, the leader of the routed band, cringed. "They are dead, Señor Velarde."

"Dead! And the *gringo* I described to you — this gunslick range dick called Joshua Dillard. He is dead also, hey?"

Mendoza trembled. "Not that I know

of. It may be, of course. We fired many shots, but we did not see him die."

Velarde regarded him fixedly, twisting a tip of his black moustachios. It seemed a very long, dangerous silence to Mendoza before the big-bellied man asked in silky tones, "What was he doing then, when last you saw him? Was he still riding to Argos City?"

"*Si, Si, señor*, he was riding in that direction," Mendoza admitted.

"And you let him go after he kill Gustavo and Miguel? Why for you do that?"

"The *jefe* is mistaken. The *hombre* Dillard was indeed very quick with his gun, and he shoot Gustavo, but the cows kill Miguel."

Velarde snarled. "Cows? *Madre de Dios!* What foolish games have you been playing, *amigo mio*?"

"Me, I play no games, my patron," Mendoza whimpered. "But the *norte-americano*, he is one crafty man, I think — "

"Did I not warn you that this Dillard

has the gun reputation? Did I not impress upon you the importance that the *buscadero* should not reach Argos City; that he should be eliminated?"

"*Si, Si . . .* " Mendoza's companions withered before Velarde's contempt, but their leader tried to plead their case. "But it could not be helped. It is as I say, he drive the herd of fevered cattle — "

At this point. Loco Louey lost his patience entirely and gave way to the callous madness which, together with his partiality for the loco weed, gave him his nickname.

Twin pistols with long barrels and notched, silver-mounted butts nestled in massive holsters on Velarde's thighs. He whipped one out and it crashed viciously.

With sick terror, Mendoza saw the flame stab from the blue-black muzzle a micro-instant before the lead smashed his right kneecap, spinning him round and collapsing him in an agonized heap on the floor.

"You are incompetent and useless, Alfonso," Velarde scorned him. his voice ugly. "There is no place for you here."

"You devil!" Mendoza gasped, all caution swept away by excruciating pain. "You have *made* me useless — you have crippled me!"

Velarde snorted, then raised his gun and fired again, this time shattering Mendoza's left knee.

"Be thankful I have not killed you, *compadre*."

★ ★ ★

Joshua Dillard came to Argos City, and was impressed by its bustle. He walked the black past the extensive cattle pens clustered around the railroad tracks east of the commercial heart and on up Main Street.

He observed the crowds thronging the plank sidewalks and the unpaved streets that were probably thoroughfares of clinging mud in winter. Traffic was continual with clopping hoofs stirring the dust and the creaking wheels of buckboards and spring-buggies scoring short-lived tracks. A plodding team of mules pulled by a laden freight wagon.

"Quite a burg." Joshua commented in a murmur.

It was laid out with more care than many of the western towns he knew, with numerous side streets all branching off the broad main drag at right angles.

Three saloons were strung along Main Street, all doing good business, and the smell of spiced food and fresh coffee had him looking in longingly through the windows of a restaurant, equally busy. His stomach fluttered hungrily. But first he had to find the livery barn and organize some lodgings for himself.

The barn was reached through an alley at the opposite end of town from the railroad depot, past the courthouse and the jail, and before the local 'boot hill' cemetery and an outlying scattering of mean shacks Joshua took to be the Mexican quarter.

After his horse was stabled, it was coming dusk and the town's lights were winking on as he footed it back to the town's centre. The Cattlemen's Commercial Bank had now shut its heavy doors, but two false-fronted general stores were still doing business, and behind the lines of saddled horses tied at the hitch racks, the walks were as humming as ever with activity. The sounds of raucous voices and a tinkling, out-of-tune piano spilled from the Broken Wheel saloon.

Joshua paused to get his bearings in the pool of flickering kerosene lamplight that spilled through the batwings.

"Stranger, are yuh?" a voice said from the gloom under the awning. An old man in the rough garb of a roustabout sat on the walk, his back against the wooden wall of the saloon, the curled brim of a battered high-crowned hat apparently tipped over his eyes.

Joshua set down his warbag and appraised the loafer. He was not one to encourage curiosity, but local knowledge picked up from idle street chatter had served him well in the past.

"Howdy, mister. What told you that?" he said laconically.

The oldster pushed back his hat and squirted tobacco juice from one corner of his mouth at a fluttering moth. He was accurate, too, bringing the thing down with a messy plop on the boards.

"Place'd be crawlin' with 'em, by God."

Joshua was not completely sure whether he meant strangers or moths. "Is that right?" He tried to sound mildly astonished.

His informant willingly rose to the bait. "Yep! This hyar bein' the county seat an' all. But that ain't the half

25

of it, no sir! Thar be more strangers 'n townfolk on account o' boss-man Maxwell's opry house, yuh savvy?"

"Oh yeah?" Joshua said questioningly.

"Fer a fact! Yuh mean t'say yuh ain't heerd?"

Joshua shrugged as though in ignorance and gave the man a lopsided smile. An hour back, he had decided to approach his mission in Argos City cautiously. Call it a hunch or what you will, but he did not think it wise to come to the table and instantly show his hand. His years of service with the famous Allan Pinkerton Detective Agency, his time since as a freelance troubleshooter, and the blows life had dealt him, had sharpened his instincts. They had also taught him shrewdness and the value of subterfuge.

The old man pressed on, enjoying his part in enlightening the only man in town who was apparently in the dark. "The town is bustin' at the seams, yuh would of see'd *that*," he said with a hint of disgust for anyone who might not. "Folks of bin a-comin' in fer miles aroun' figgerin' t' see this French actin' dame — " he hesitated as his whiskery jaws wrapped themselves around the foreign name — this Gisèle Bourdette an her play-actin' comp'ny."

"You mean here — in Argos City?"

"I suttinly do, stranger! Argos City ain't no one-hoss town no more. It's grow'd up — thanks t' Big Ben, I guess."

"Big Ben?"

"Bennett Maxwell. He's the richest man hereabouts. Rode roughshod in the fifties an' sixties an' built up the richest spread in this hyar country. When the grabbin' was good, he grabbed most ev'rythin' in sight! But he's respect'ble now, y'unnerstand? Hankers t' be seen as a pillar o' the community." The old man cackled at secret thoughts. "Big wheels don't never know when t' stop rollin'. Spent seventy thousand dollars on erectin' the opry house, would yuh b'lieve!"

Joshua was getting the picture and

27

was glad he had not begrudged the ancient gossip his time. Maxwell had been mentioned in the letter he had received in Saltillo from New York — but not in these interesting terms.

"Seventy thousand is a hell of a lot of greenbacks," he said. Even in the business district, most of the buildings Joshua had seen were graceless, utilitarian structures, put up in all the haste of a typical cattle town boom. The courthouse had a modest dignity, yet saloons and gambling halls stood cheek by jowl, looking positively jerry-built. Clapboard, adobe and rock-and-adobe were the predominant materials.

Seventy thousand dollars spent in this milieu stretched credibility.

But the gabby native nodded his head. "Banker Cartwright reckoned the same, folks says, but Big Ben had th' loot, an' he's still high-handed an' mulish. Drags a lot o' weight. I figger he's fixin' on runnin' th' politics o' town an county mighty soon. He'll be usin' this hyar Frenchie actress to elevate hisself in the public eye — t' show Argos City is on the map, thanks to his high-toned opry house."

"A patron of the arts and public benefactor . . . " Joshua mused.

"Yeah, a benny — " The old timer gave up on it. "What yuh says, mister."

Joshua could fill in more of the details from his own knowledge and imagination.

Deadwood, Dakota, had its Gem Theatre. Tombstone, Arizona, had its Bird Cage — like many mining town playhouses, the adjunct of a saloon. In Virginia City, Nevada, and Central City, Colorado, as in Argos City, the theatres were called opera houses, although little if any opera was heard in them; it was just that the frontier communities reckoned the term 'opera house' was more suggestive of culture and class.

From the beginning, the theatre was an accustomed part of American life. A sign of a cow town's or mining town's maturity was its building of a playhouse. Where life was hard and rugged, diversion of all kinds did a roaring business. Audiences were avid for any form of entertainment, and Joshua had seen them take their seats for the classics as happily as for the variety shows. Shakespearian drama seemed never to pall, even with a public that often had only rudimentary book learning. Season after season, the tragedies in particular were performed to an appreciative reception wherever strolling players ventured.

"Yuh be lookin' fer someplace t' rest up, stranger?" the old man cut into Joshua's thoughts. "Spare beds'd be purty hard to find. Ev'ry damn one's filled with a drama stoodent!" He laughed at his sarcasm. "Not thet many of 'em kin foller French, but they heerd how these Paris actresses make their way, an' how in France it ain't no stigma. They see'd this Bourdette woman's pitcher, an' now they jest wanna see the body in the flesh an' think about what they'd like t' do with her!"

Joshua could appreciate what stimulated the old timer's bawdy thoughts. The common belief was that French actresses were without exception courtesans. It need not necessarily be true they were all members of that other profession, but it was put around that they were not insulted when invited to bed in appropriate circumstances. Indeed, the reward for sexual favours could be significant in the right cases. Moreover, a large percentage of highly placed and intelligent Frenchmen of the time openly regarded the courtesan as the ideal woman. Many French books had cocottes as their heroines.

"If Gisèle Bourdette wouldn't be good t' sleep with, I don't know nothin' 'bout women!" Joshua's informant cackled lewdly before pulling himself together. "Howsumever, this don't git yuh no place to bunk down, mister."

"What do you suggest?" Joshua asked.

The man pretended to cogitate. "The hotel's packed, but yuh c'd try Ma Hoadley's boarding house," he said, as though this was a brilliantly original thought. "I happen t' know thet a feller left recent an' his room was empty yesterday. Kinda small, mind, an' up in th' attic. But it's awright, I tell yuh — a mighty genteel establishment, an' close to the middle o' town."

Joshua told the garrulous old fellow he would drift along and got the address. He dug in his coat pocket, rewarded him with a fresh plug of tobacco and headed off.

"Say — tell Ma Hoadley ol' Joe sent yuh aroun'!"

Mrs Hoadley was a formidable operator, with a round, moonlike face, several chins and well-muscled, sleeveless arms. "Sure, I've got a room for a gentleman," she said, casting a critical eye over him. "Four dollars fifty a night."

After some haggling, Dillard secured the room at a rent of two fifty a night, or fifteen dollars a week. It was as well he argued.

The room the big woman showed him to, under the roof rafters at the top of her spotless house, was the merest cubbyhole and had been intended by its builder either as a box-room or a place for a child to sleep. There would be just about enough room for Joshua to stand by the narrow truckle bed and change his clothes.

"Well, no matter," he consoled himself. "It should be a room with a view."

He crossed the creaking, polished floor in one stride and peered out through the chintz-curtained window into the fading light.

He gulped. "Good God almighty!"

His gaze had been instantly drawn to the gap between the roofs of two facing buildings. What he saw beyond them was like something out of Ancient Greece.

3

Miss Maxwell is Unwilling

RANCHER Bennett Maxwell loved best to see his only child dressed in range clothes. Expensive stuff, of course. A coloured blouse beneath a doeskin waistcoat and a fringed, divided skirt with beaded pockets. And around her shapely hips, a neat cartridge belt with a small, pearl-handled .38 in a tooled holster . . . Then, slender and straight but fully matured at nineteen, she looked every inch a capable frontierswoman and he could easily forget his regrets that she had not been born a boy to carry on his family name when she inherited the vast B-Bar-M spread.

But tonight she was dressed in another image which, beautiful and admittedly fitting though it was, did not at heart afford him so complete a pleasure.

They were at their town house, brick-built and solid in the most select residential quarter of Argos City where it had replaced a humbler, clapboard structure which had been part of the original town.

Lorena Maxwell was wearing a beautiful gown of gleaming gold silk trimmed with red at the cuffs and the deep neckline. Its draped skirt fell from the nipped-in waist to the floor in shimmering folds, hiding a pair of trim ankles and tiny feet. Her hair was dressed in glossy black ringlets and tied with ribbons of scarlet satin.

"Wonderful, my dear," Maxwell said, thrusting his thumbs under the lapels of his broadcloth suit coat. His chest swelled with pride under the heavy gold watch chain across his braided vest. "I'm mighty glad I had that dress sent all the way from Kansas City. But don't you think you might of saved its first wearin' fer when you go to the opera house tomorrow with Colby Vane?"

"No, I do not!" his pretty daughter snapped. Her face seemed to darken beneath the duskiness of her Texas-tanned complexion and her jet eyes flashed. She looked for a moment every inch her father's child. Along with her feminine perfection came the same hint of determination in the firmness of the chin.

"I needed to try it out first," she said more reasonably. "And we do have a dinner guest tonight, you will remember."

The rancher scowled like a sulky schoolboy despite being a tall, balding man of big build and fiftysome years. "The better reason not to show off your finery a day early, child."

"Oh, fiddlesticks! One New Yorker will see it — no one else in Argos City." Lorena was stiff-backed, full of angry dignity. She came to the reason why.

"Your precious Colby Vane will never

know he wasn't honoured to gaze upon it first."

"Now don't get on your high horse with me, Lorena. Colby is a fine, respectable young feller, bred to the range — "

"Tchah!" Her red lips lost their softness in the expression of her impatience. Being a Maxwell also meant she was one of the few unafraid of Big Ben; rumour had it this pair would on occasion spit and scream at one another like wildcats. "I do wish you'd stop throwing me at the boy's head, Pa. I know very well his father is one of your cattlemen cronies and president of the Stock Association, but a girl might just want to follow her own inclinations and set her sights someplace else!"

"Now, Lorena, be sensible. If you suppose I've got anythin' but your best interests at heart, you're mistaken. You know you can't set them sights any higher 'n the son of Gulliver Vane."

Lorena bluntly spoke her mind.

37

"That's what *you* might think, Father! But it so happens there are things more important than cattle-raising and making money. Hogtying myself so I can some day be a rich rancher's wife doesn't appeal to me."

Maxwell had large curving moustaches with the fine sweep of a bull's horns. They quivered in their iron-grey magnificence and behind them, his jaw clenched. "So what does?"

"I want to get away from here — go someplace, be something and enjoy life . . . I'm afraid my ideas about myself don't tally up to marrying Colby Vane until I've had a good look round first."

"Plumb crazy notions, child! Your poor mother would turn in her grave if she could hear you speak them."

"Well, it's true, so I may as well say it. I can't abide Colby Vane making up to me — getting right fresh, no matter his respectability. To please you, Pa, I'm allowing him to escort me to the opera house to see Gisèle

Bourdette. But don't try to finagle me into marrying him — because I won't finagle worth a hoot!"

They glowered at each other for a hard moment, then Big Ben relented. For a fact, some folk said Lorena was the only one who could wrap her old man around her little finger. When it came to close kin, she was all he'd had since his wife had died in Lorena's early childhood. "All right, Lorena, I hear what you say." He shook his great head sadly. "You look all growed up, but there's a ways to go afore you'll see Maxwell horse sense, I guess."

Lorena loosened up, laughing playfully, the merriment putting lights into her liquid-dark eyes. "Since I've never been a filly, and unless you see yourself as a stallion, Daddy dear, that's plain ridiculous!"

But they were a tricky pair; even though their quarrel might have looked a clear-cut conflict of ambitions, neither was levelling with the other.

Back of Maxwell's concerns for his

daughter's future security lay deep worries he had not voiced even to her. On the eve of an event which would remind the populace he was the prominent citizen who had built the city's magnificent opera house, he should rightly have been brimming with the pleasure of his life's ostensible success. Yet it was not so. He had gotten himself into one hell of a tangle and the severity of the problems he kept perforce to himself threatened to destroy his enjoyment of the occasion.

Meanwhile, Lorena's excuse for donning her stunning new clothes was not her true motive — that was something she had not yet dared to admit even to herself. It centred on the very recent arrival in Argos City of one Edward Carter Jnr, of New York City.

Carter, everyone knew, was the adventurous young American impresario organising the tour by Gisèle Bourdette and her company. At age twenty-eight, he was already a brilliant operator. having largely taken over the New York,

Paris and London theatrical agency founded by his father — 'the Chief', now kept to his bed in Manhattan by failing health.

Currently, Carter Jnr was carefully managing the endless publicity which so delighted the French actress and was ensuring her financial success in the New World. He had arrived in Argos City several days ahead of the troupe to finalise arrangements for the performance at Bennett Maxwell's opera house.

With his Eastern accent, silk-lined cape, waistcoat in flowered brocade and mane of wavy blond hair, Edward Carter was also the undeniable possessor of a clean-shaven, boyish charm that quickened Lorena's heartbeat.

He was handsome; he was cosmopolitan. He had instantly brought the outside world to the wide open but oddly confining spaces of Lorena's Western existence.

And tonight he was their dinner guest.

***

"I must say," said Edward Carter Jnr, chewing with relish another morsel cut from the juicy steak on his plate. "You do raise a prime grade of beef, Mr Maxwell."

Bennett Maxwell dabbed at his moustache with a lawn table napkin. "Much obliged to hear it, Mr Carter. Raisin' beeves is my business. I've been introducin' the American breeds here, you know — Shorthorns, Herefords, Devons. There's no doubt even Texans prefer the higher quality beef, but we still run mostly Longhorns, which are, of course, of Spanish or Mexican origin."

Lorena, the third seated at the big round table, laughed lightly and turned her eyes on Carter, which was something she was far from loath to do. She'd already noted the young impresario was immaculate from his well-groomed head of hair to his patent leather footwear. He wore a superb suit of quality English cloth and cut, and his linen shirt was spotlessly white.

"You mustn't let father bore you with his shop talk, Mr Carter," Lorena told him.

"Don't be silly. Lorena," Maxwell said. "Mr Carter is a businessman himself. A different business, for sure. But he'll appreciate the importance of practical considerations. Yes, indeedy! And if I hadn't prospered as a cattleman, Argos City would have no playhouse where he could bring his artistes."

In truth, Lorena knew her father wouldn't see much alike with the stranger at his table. She imagined he was faintly suspicious of his smooth manners and his fancy Dan clothes. And he'd be irritated by the phantom whiff of pomade that hung about his blond waves, whereas she was only intrigued.

But his belief in Carter as a talented and formidable manager of business affairs would be sincere — and correct.

"I must say," said Carter, "I never expected to find so magnificent a theatre at the back-end of nowhere."

Lorena had already noted the list of things the personable Easterner 'must say' was extensive; it seemed a kind of deferential, all-purpose prefix to so many of his perceptive comments. Why she didn't find it irritating was a question that hadn't so much as occurred to her.

"As a matter of fact, I had grave reservations about including Argos City on the Bourdette Special's itinerary," Carter went on. "Some opinion has it your town is — uh — wide open. Mr Maxwell. Worse than Tombstone, Arizona . . . its environs a home to desperadoes from across the Border."

A look that Lorena read peculiarly like alarm flitted across her father's face, narrowing and brightening his eyes to steely points. Then Big Ben shrugged irritably.

"Don't heed no rumours, Mr Carter. I reckon that special train will be as safe here as anyplace, you hear?"

Maxwell gestured with a large hand, encompassing the opulence of the richly gleaming, polished furnishings, the gilt-framed pictures and heavy drapes, as though the very room vouchsafed sanctuary for a continent-pounding locomotive and the cars it pulled.

Carter looked like he was wondering what made his host bluster so. Perhaps, like Lorena did herself, he put it down to home-town pride.

"Well, never mind, Mr Maxwell. It's too late for me to reschedule the tour now. Besides, my pa has engaged an ex-Pinkerton detective to join the touring party here in an advisory capacity and ensure its safe progress.

Maxwell snapped gruffly, "That Joshua Dillard feller!"

"Dillard was the name. The Chief gave me to understand he has a hatred of lawbreakers and a reputation in localities renowned for wildness."

"Ha!" Maxwell snorted. "Your pa wrote me, too, but these gunfighter

45

types don't cut no ice with me, I tell you." His tone was heavy with distaste. "Dillard is a *killer*, no better than the riffraff he hounds for bounty. The way I heard it, he was thrown out of the Pinkerton agency in disgrace."

"I don't think so, Mr Maxwell," Carter courteously informed the testy rancher. "I understand his resignation followed the murder of his wife by the Wilder gang in San Antonio, Texas."

Maxwell brushed aside the explanation. "Well, whatever! We don't need his likes sneakin' around in Argos City." An unheralded draught stirred the close air in the room and he seemed to brighten as though some other thought had occurred to him. "It's no important matter anyhow, I guess, since the odds are ten to one he won't show up."

Carter frowned. "Why do you say that? The Chief gave me to understand Dillard is a drifter, but reliable once he commits himself."

Maxwell leaned back in his chair and shrugged. "Lots of attractions to keep a feller of Dillard's stripe busy down in Messico . . . immunity from the law, cheap livin', pretty *señoritas*, fer a start."

Carter did not question Maxwell's opinion, but only because he was denied the rancher's attention — and even Lorena's — by what happened next.

The floor-length window curtains, which had billowed gently in the draught of a moment before, were suddenly swept aside and a fourth person was present in the room. Behind him, a raised sash showed how he had slipped in. While the occupants had talked, he had hooked fingers under the partly open window and noiselessly lifted it high.

"Good evening, gents!" the newcomer said.

"Who the hell are you?" Maxwell yelped, leaping to his feet. So great was his consternation, he also unwisely went to draw the long Colt that made a bulge under his coat tails.

The stranger instantly beat his move and Maxwell stared dumbfounded into the black muzzle of the .45 Peacemaker that had appeared from nowhere into the man's fist. Lorena guessed it was as fast a draw as her father had ever seen; he froze mid-lunge. Fear flicked across his eyes.

"Dillard," the gun-handy intruder stated. "The name's Joshua Dillard." With his free hand he pulled a sheaf of crumpled letters from an inner pocket and tossed them on the table amidst the glittering silver cutlery and crystal glassware. "These are my credentials."

Carter's eyes alighted on his company's New York letterhead and his father's own handwriting on one of the sheets, and he broke the tension with a roar of laughter.

"You are very good with that gun, Mr Dillard, but you about scared the hell out of us!"

Bennett Maxwell agreed, but with a truculence that was not in the younger man. "Too damned good with the gun," he growled. "And how come you're bustin' into my house like this, mister? There's no call fer it!"

Dillard gave his gun a twirl by the trigger guard before holstering it. He looked away from Maxwell's antagonistic stare and winked at Lorena and Edward Carter.

"Sounded to me like there's every call, Mr Maxwell, seeing how convinced you are your little burg is a safe place for Mr Carter's visiting player-queen. What say I was a thief or a crank? I've myself lately sidestepped a bushwhacking by a mess of local *bandoleros* not more'n an hour's ride south."

Carter said, "He's right, you know. Why should a theatrical troupe be safe from renegades and outlaws when a gunman can walk right into the house of a prominent citizen?"

Maxwell scowled. "I'll have a crew of my top hands ride in from the B-Bar-M directly. They'll be put at the disposal of the town marshal."

Joshua shook his head. "The town's chock-full already. Another passel of cow-men sitting it out in town would prob'ly get half-drunk. If'n a greaser wolf-pack rode in, they'd be like to go off half-cocked and fall over the rest!"

"What do you suggest then?" Maxwell retorted.

"To my way of thinking, your illustrious guest and her party should be spoken to plain about how it is, and revolvers should be distributed to every man in the troupe. I could arrange some practice shooting."

Maxwell's hands clenched into tight fists and his whole body stiffened. "Revolvers!" the rancher snapped. "Hell, mister, have you seen my theatre? It's a place for *culture*, not a damned shooting gallery!"

"Yeah, I seen your playhouse — from an upstairs window at a rooming-house. It looked like a Greek temple to me, what with them sandstone pillars and fancy masonry. But robber bands respect only one god — money.

Which ain't a good thing, seeing that place sure reeks of it, and it'd attract 'em like buzzards to spoiled meat, even without a top actress."

Carter sided with Dillard. "It makes sense, Mr Maxwell. We'll arm the players soon as they arrive tomorrow morning."

Lorena's father had fought enough battles in his time to know when he had won or lost. It went badly with him, but she saw he had to concede Dillard's point or look a mite crazy. He paced the room and looked out the window into the darkening night.

"All right, we'll do it your way — let 'em have guns."

His voice was rougher than a file on broken-edged iron.

4

Hellfire Welcome

"IT'S a damned insult, Lorena. Our town is playing host to a world-famous celebrity and the shots are being called by a bloody gunfighter!"

Bennett Maxwell had spent a restless night. Eaten up by his anger at Joshua Dillard's interference in what he perceived to be *his* affairs, sleep had been a long time coming, and when he eventually awakened it seemed he had slept only a few minutes, whereas it had in fact been several hours.

Now, breakfasted, bathed and his magnificent moustaches carefully waxed, his cheeks burned brick-red beneath the broad brim of a new white Stetson as he bottled up his indignation and drove his neat spring buggy onto Main Street, headed for the railroad depot. His grip on the ribbons made his knuckles show white.

It was a beautiful day. With the morning sun already riding high, the streets should normally have been next to empty at this time; the town should have looked quiet and lazy with activity confined to the hushed cool of the veranda-covered plankwalks. But today was something of a holiday. Folks decked out in their Sunday best were drifting on down in excited bunches to the railyards.

"Oh, do unwind, dad," Maxwell's beautiful daughter said, seated beside him under the shade of a parasol. "I'm sure Mr Dillard and Edward never meant to get your back up. It's just your pride that's hurt."

Stung, Maxwell defended himself by going on the attack.

"*Edward,*" he sneered. "I see you've gotten farther than just making sheep eyes at Carter then."

Lorena blushed furiously. "Now you're

being ridiculous, daddy," she protested. "I must say — *I do declare* all this excitement is getting you wrought up!"

If Maxwell noticed his daughter had caught herself copying the phrase so liberally employed by the New Yorker, he did not specifically comment on it. "H'mph. Well, remember this, gal, Carter won't be on our map for long, and he won't give a tinker's cuss for no Texas rancher's daughter." Another worry stabbed at him. "By glory, it'll be a bad thing if the Vanes see you making up to that dude Easterner! If Gulliver Vane thinks his son is being slighted . . . "

"I'm sorry, father. I meant what I said last night. Colby Vane means nothing to me, and I do wish you would stop insinuating it will ever be to the contrary."

It was perhaps as well the buggy ride was only a short one and the chance for private words soon ended. Lorena was prepared to do most things her father asked and would try hard not to buck him. But there were limits to what could be expected of the most dutiful daughter. She resolved to let matters take their course, to keep a clear head and to have no more contact with the odious Colby Vane than was absolutely necessary.

Under the auspices of an *ad hoc* reception committee of Argos City's leading townspeople, an area had been roped off adjacent to the railroad depot's platform. As befitted a man of standing and substance, and the builder of the opera house that made the occasion possible, Bennett Maxwell was ushered with his daughter into the reserved space. where other dignitaries were already assembled in their finery.

In spite of herself, Lorena's eyes sought out Mr Edward Carter Jnr and dwelled upon him, liquid soft. Notwithstanding the heat and the environment, he wore a frock coat, a top hat, white shirt and white stiff collar, with a colourful silk tie. When he spotted Lorena and her father, he swept his hat from his handsome head and bowed gracefully.

"I must say you are the most refreshing sight I've seen all morning, Miss Maxwell," he complimented her.

★ ★ ★

The embarrassment into which Carter's compliment put the young woman, and how she cast her eyes to the ground, masking their too-obvious secrets with black-lashed lids, was jealously observed by Colby Vane.

The son of the president of the county's Stock Association was a strapping youth, well over six feet tall and broad-shouldered to boot with a square, humourless face and deep-set grey eyes beneath sandy brows. A sneer tweaked the corners of his thick lips as he haughtily contemplated what he thought of as the foppish stranger.

But it put his nose out of joint to see the eloquent self-consciousness with which Lorena Maxwell carried her slenderly delectable form under the man's watch.

Of course, the girl was likely only to make a fool of herself. His father, Gulliver, had it from Bennett Maxwell himself, who was kind of hosting this whole galling charade, that the fellow Carter was totally obsessed by his work as a theatrical impresario.

In particular, it seemed Carter really himself believed all the puffery that had been printed in the various states' newspapers and treated the touring French actress Gisèle Bourdette like she was a goddess. His worship, and determination to make the best provision possible for the great woman's comfort and safety while she was in America, could surely be counted on to make him blind to just about most else — including Lorena Maxwell.

So Colby Vane gritted his teeth and purposefully set his mind to thinking about the day that would surely come when the pretty Lorena would be his to play with as he liked, which was how it was with most things that took his privileged fancy.

★ ★ ★

Lorena's father slapped the Vanes, father and son, on the back. What was evidently the whole town and most of the county was assembling at the depot, but Joshua Dillard being nowhere in sight, Maxwell had assumed his most expansive mood and was handing out foreign cigars.

"Howdy, Gulliver, Colby — here, try one of these. They're mighty fine stogies!"

Gulliver Vane, a normally dour man a head shorter than his son but built on the same broad lines, chomped the end off his free smoke and reached for a match. "This hyar must be a proud occasion fer yuh, Big Ben. Guess they'll be nominatin' yuh fer Argos City mayor come next elections."

Maxwell did not get to acknowledge

this agreeable accolade before the distant clanging of a brass engine bell and the wail of a steam whistle announced the approach of the special train. Excitement buzzed through the crowd and necks were craned as people strained to glimpse the dark-red speck and the tower of smoke down the tracks.

"It's just like the circus coming to town!" Lorena said.

At this same moment, the Reverend Abraham Toole also chose to make his presence felt. Toole was the minister of the cow-town's Baptist church — a tall, cadaverous man with disapproval etched permanently in the lines of his face, and a grave voice that reverberated like an echo from a tomb.

Toole was a preacher in the fire-and-brimstone mould and had a devoted following among certain of the town's ladies. Those who didn't notice he was long on misery but short on charity, Lorena categorized them. He strode out in front of the crowd and standing with his back to the very edge of the tracks began to harangue the assembly.

"Brothers, sisters, you witness the coming of the engine of Satan! Let us recognize it for the scarlet coloured beast of the Scriptures." He opened a well-thumbed Bible at a marked page and waved it before the noses of his boggling audience. "Upon it rides the mother of harlots, decked with gold and precious stones and pearls, having a golden cup in her hand full of abominations and filthiness of her fornication!"

Toole, evidently, had read the newspapers, too. Many column inches had been filled on the subject of Gisèle Bourdette. There had been sketches of her gowns on the women's pages. descriptions of her Paris home, and her opinions on everything from cosmetics to Molière. But most of the advance publicity, including that in the pages of the *Argos City Press*, had been devoted to the scandalous and indiscriminate nature of her love-life.

"This *whore* has been sent to destroy the morals of American citizens!" Toole intoned wrathfully. He flipped through the pages of his Bible. "Return to your homes, for a whore is a deep ditch; and a strange woman is a narrow pit. She also lieth in wait as for a prey, and increaseth the transgressors among men!"

Maxwell groaned. "The stupid old fart will ruin everything!"

"Father!" Lorena hissed in reproof.

"Be not tempted with her wicked smile and promises of sin! The harbingers of vice must not be allowed to sully our fair city!" exhorted Toole.

"Shut him up, someone!" Maxwell bleated tersely.

Edward Carter appeared at his side, smiling. "Don't get too riled up, Mr Maxwell. It happens all over. The Bishop of Chicago pronounced an anathema upon Gisèle and all her immoral works. I must say it ensured us capacity audiences and enormous receipts!"

Maxwell continued to fume despite Carter's confidence. "I can remember Preacher Toole fifteen years back, before he Got The Call. Abe was a hard-drinking, crib-haunting, two-fisted range rider. Now the stinking coyote's swallowed so much religion it's warped all his other figurings. It's a confounded insult to me, that's what it is!"

From things he'd let slip, Lorena knew her father was at bottom very mindful that the methods by which he had amassed his wealth had not included reading his Bible, saying his prayers and regularly attending church. Far from it, if rumour were to be believed.

The speck down the tracks had become larger and larger until the great steam-belching locomotive and the cars it pulled were braking to a walking pace preparatory to their triumphal entry into the Argos City depot.

Along the platform a French tricolour was unfurled and raised and a band struck up *La Marseillaise*. The band began to march, moving toward the tracks.

"Hey! The band ain't supposed to *march* anyplace, for God's sake!" Maxwell said.

Carter's eyebrows raised, too, but then he saw something that Maxwell had not.

"It's not for God's sake, Mr Maxwell, but for the sake of his high-handed advocate, I reckon! If you look closely, you'll see Joshua Dillard amidst the bandsmen with a drawn revolver. He'll whip your sky pilot into line!"

The band proceeded up the platform and engulfed Abraham Toole. Obscured from all but the sharpest eyes, which included Lorena's, the preacher was hustled along with the procession, persuasively prodded in his bony ribs by Dillard's Peacemaker.

"A Babylon harlot . . . She that profanes herself by playing the whore shall be burnt with fire!" Toole declaimed. But even his booming tones were no match for the Argos City brass and his last rant was drowned out.

"Oh, nice work, Mr Dillard!" Lorena exclaimed, her brown eyes bright.

"He can't hear you, Lorena," her father said with what she thought was ungrateful gruffness.

"I know *that*," the girl muttered chiefly to herself.

The dark-red, shiny-trimmed locomotive clanked noisily past the waiting crowd and drew to a squealing halt, bringing its three grand cars to a standstill alongside the platform. These cars, constructed in Chicago by George Mortimer Pullman's famous Palace Car Company, were done out like first-class hotels.

Eager eyes, trying to glimpse the luxury and the celebrated travellers within, searched the windows framed by rich curtains, green and crimson and interwoven with gold. As recently as 1877 more miles of railroad track had been laid in Texas during the year than in any other state, but Lorena and

Argos City had never seen the like of rolling-stock as magnificent as this.

A uniformed black steward appeared on the rear deck of the last car and hooked back a door, then the great actress herself made her entrance.

Mademoiselle Bourdette was a smaller woman than Lorena had expected, but she radiated her presence. Lorena could imagine her stepping onto a stage. The tragedienne might also look frail and tired, with a delicate skin, but her hazel eyes, rather narrow and tending upward at the outer corners, gave her a feline alertness. Lorena, even in her limited experience, suspected men might find this alluring and the effect, she conceded herself, was not entirely unpleasant.

Was it a breath of wind or the simultaneous gasp of the agog populace that stirred the air behind the ranch girl?

Gisèle Bourdette's gown was the very latest thing in striped royal-blue silk and gossamer-like muslin and lace. It had a gracefully flowing skirt and a high waistline that made the woman look taller than she actually was. The bodice was close-fitting and the whole was clearly innocent of any foundation of whalebone construction.

Long lace gloves concealed her hands and arms, which also carried a great many gold and jewelled bangles. A scarf of diaphanous material, edged with silver, was wound loosely around her neck.

With a queenly elegance, she stepped down from the train's rear deck onto the platform and offered her hand to Argos City's slope-shouldered mayor, Ward Hastie, who did not know quite what to do with it. He was rescued from his tongue-tied embarrassment by the immediate approach of a small child with a huge bunch of flowers.

Gisèle's clinging gown shimmered in the sunlight as she bent down, easily and gracefully, to accept the tribute.

"Merci . . . Thank you. I am pleased to arrive and you are most kind."

She spoke English intelligibly, if not fluently. Edward Carter said, "That accent! Isn't it charming? I must say it's the most adorable thing I ever heard."

Lorena felt the stab of what she recognized was jealousy, no less, and cursed herself for a fool.

Fortunately, there was no need for her to reply to the admiring impresario. The crowd cheered Gisèle's few words with as much enthusiasm as if they were a passionately delivered speech in a moving drama.

And the band launched again into *La Marseillaise* with redoubled vigour, many of the musicians hitting false notes in their zeal.

5

A Gun for Gisèle

THE welcoming ceremony was thankfully wrapped up inside half an hour. A long line of celebrity seekers, whom Gisèle Bourdette had found provincial and unsophisticated, had pressed in on her to gush over her and pump her hand till the rings cut into her fingers. 'Le handshake' was very trying, she told Edward Carter when she was finally allowed to retreat to her Palace car, now shunted into a siding where it was to act as a hotel.

"Mademoiselle, we must not discourage your public wherever and howsoever we find them," Carter said. "I must say you at least were spared a confrontation with another hellfire-ranting preacherman." He gestured towards one of the other three people in the luxurious saloon. "By Mr Joshua Dillard here."

"Ah, but you say all publicity is good publicity, Edward." Gisèle pronounced the name Edw-ah-d. "Tell me about it."

While Carter recounted the story of how Abraham Toole got his come-uppance, Gisèle appraised Dillard with a frank, exploring stare.

She saw a weathered, hard-faced man with pale blue eyes — not cold but unsmiling and, she sensed, forever marked with the reflection of some deep and scarring tragedy. Careless of his surroundings evidently, he wore rough range garb and toted a Colt six-shooter with a black butt worn from use; the grip she could see actually appeared cracked. He towered above her, standing tall, his back straight as a ramrod and his head held erectly above broad shoulders.

"The Chief has sent Mr Dillard to join our party and be our protector in the Wild West," Carter finished. "Mr

Dillard has a reputation as a trouble-shooter. I must say he can handle a gun as well as Wes Hardin or Wild Bill Hickok!"

Gisèle was intrigued. Whatever his accomplishments, Mr Dillard, in his faded, well-worn clothes and with dark stubble on his chin, had the general appearance of a saddle tramp down on his luck. But for all that, very capable. She smiled at him. "I can see you are a man who is not — what is it that you say? — easily rattled."

"Sure, ma'am, but we've got other fat to chew. This talking about me ain't getting us no place." His voice was quiet and pleasant, but there was a brusqueness in it, too.

Gisèle, who believed in self-advertisement and delighted in it, performed a mock pout. "Oh, but there is only one thing worse than being talked about, and that is *not* being talked about."

Carter laughed. "Mademoiselle is quoting the famous Oscar Wilde, you know," he said for Joshua's information.

"Wilde is the Irish dramatist who lectured Colorado miners from the stage of the Tabor Opera House, Leadville, on the Ethics of Art."

"Yeah ... and he held a single white lily in his hand, I heard tell. Sounds plumb crazy to me. The feller sure has gotten the wrong handle in Wilde. I figure your actors should carry *guns*, Mr Carter, not any damned *flowers*."

Gisèle shivered, not because she was afraid at this prospect but because she was excited by it.

"Is it not thrilling, Henri? I am so glad we included the frontier land on our *grande voyage*!"

The handsome young man she addressed scowled, his face reddening with anger.

"You are glad that we should have to carry shooting-irons and be bossed by a savage lout, mademoiselle?"

"Hey, watch your lip, mister!" Joshua objected.

With his fringe of golden hair and

clean-cut features, Henri Rabier-Roget was built like a Roman god, but a tic in his cheek hinted at an instability in his character. Clearly he resented Joshua, the more so because of the unconcealed, bold-eyed interest he was receiving from Gisele.

"I will not take orders from a mercenary ruffian, even if he is the fastest gunhand in the American West!" he snarled, showing his even white teeth.

Joshua unbuckled his gunbelt. The rig thudded to the thick Turkish carpet, and he began calmly removing his coat. "Mister, if you're itching to clash with me, I'm more'n ready to oblige!"

"Gentlemen, please!" Carter intervened. "There's no call for us to hunt trouble in camp."

Joshua shrugged doubtfully, but thought better of pushing the matter to a reckoning and kept his shabby coat on his back. "It's your show, Carter, but I don't like this feller's tone."

"I must say his remarks are ill-informed, but Monsieur Rabier-Roget is the company's leading man and naturally his responsibilities weigh heavily upon him," Carter excused the good-looking French actor. "Riding a train for several months is apt to be a tiring business, too, I guess. The troupe follows a busy schedule. Evening performances begin at eight and end at eleven, then like as not it's time to start out for the next destination, travelling from midnight until morning, or sometimes until noon."

"Edward is correct," Gisèle added, treating Joshua to her most bewitching smile. "Sometimes the minute we arrive we go straight to the theatre to rehearse — and we have to set up the lighting and the scenery and the props, you understand?"

Joshua grunted acceptance of the explanation. but it looked like he would have preferred an apology from Henri Rabier-Roget's own lips, now thinned into a sneer of hatred. Perhaps he suspected — and rightly — that there was more to the actor's surly opposition than met the eye.

Gisèle felt no compulsion to make excuses for Rabier-Roget. Her status in latter years had conferred upon her the privilege of disdaining discretion or manipulation. In fact, she had never had an aptitude for either during her unrestrained career. But she did desire the grim Westerner Joshua Dillard to regard her in a favourable light.

She was a woman of catholic appetites, and despite his harshness, Dillard fascinated her. He was so unlike all other men of her very thorough acquaintance — the mighty male egos of France's Second Empire, whose patronage had sustained her during her courtesan years, and the elegant but jaded butterflies of the liberal arts scene in Paris.

Gisèle had quickly decided that she wanted to know this Joshua better. Very much better. He promised to be an exciting, refreshing experience for a *demi-mondaine*.

But she realized this would not go down at all well with Henri. In truth, pure jealousy, not tiredness, was already the mainspring of Rabier-Roget's hostility to Joshua Dillard. It had been understood for years that Bourdette's co-stars were also her lovers, and M. Rabier-Roget was the only actor in the company who shared the deluxe accommodation of her personal railroad car. The rest had quarters in the two other cars, not so sumptuously appointed.

Henri was no great actor, but he was undeniably an attractive hunk of masculinity. That had had much to do with his recruitment, and along with shared accommodation and endless private rehearsals of key scenes, he also naturally spent his off-duty time with her.

An *affaire* with Joshua Dillard, if it could be contrived, promised to create a ticklish situation, but this did not daunt Gisèle. She was

Henri's employer, after all. Taking on a handsome young unknown with the pitiful salary of six thousand francs a year was a carnal diversion, a luxury Gisèle, the successful actress-manager, felt she could afford, but not one that should restrict her freedom to exercise her tigerish sexuality.

Furthermore, Henri was proving something of a liability. His rural Brittany background made him more than a whit narrow-minded wherever his own satisfaction was not involved, and he had that curse of the age the morphine habit, which was inclined to make him moody and unpredictable.

"Maybe we should hand out the guns right off, ma'am," Joshua Dillard said, jerking Gisèle's thoughts back to the present.

"You're running things now, Mr Dillard," Carter said. "It should be howsoever you say."

Joshua shook his head. "Your pa hired me to make sure things run smooth," he argued. "You and Mademoiselle

Bourdette are still the bosses."

"Gisèle, *s'il vous plaît.*" the actress murmured, producing a fresh scowl from Henri. "And yes, let us have the guns!"

"They're right outside, packed in a wooden crate from the local gunsmith's," Carter put in. "I must say Maxwell has done us proud. Mr Dillard. Clearly he had a change of heart after our — uh — few words. He has purchased the stock of handguns for the company's use out of his own money."

Joshua rubbed the stubble on his chin raspingly, thoughtfully. "Such generosity! I guess he didn't want to be upstaged in front of his important new actor friends." There was a slightly sarcastic overtone in his voice and a glint of hard amusement in his faded eyes.

"Marie!" Gisèle addressed the fifth person in the saloon. "Go find some men to bring in the box, please."

Madame Marie Guisard instantly emerged from her unobtrusive place in the shadows and shuffled off to attend to her mistress' bidding. An aged widow, she was an old friend of Gisèle's *cocotte* mother, was devoted to attending the younger woman, and had accompanied her as servant-cum-companion for most of her tempestuous adult life.

"Madame Guisard is a treasure, Joshua," Gisèle purred. "And so able. Of course, she is old and not the beauty regular, but she is very clever. I say she is not just a treasure, she is my treasurer!" Gisèle laughed herself at this felicity, knowing it demonstrated her own cleverness with a foreign language."

Joshua frowned. "Your treasurer?"

"Mais oui! Edward tells me I have quaint whims about money. I do not trust the banks, you see. I trust my Marie."

A shadow of uneasiness flitted across Joshua's face, displacing his brooding expression. "That old lady looks after your money?" he probed.

Gisèle laughed again. "Of course! Until it is counted and has gone into the safe with my finest jewels."

"The safe?"

"It is here, with *cher* Victor!" Gisèle tugged aside a Persian hanging behind a divan piled with satin cushions. A green metal cabinet was revealed. On it stood a plaster bust of Victor Hugo.

Joshua wasn't impressed. "Ma'am — Gisèle — I guess the cheques from box-offices would be safe enough, but to my practised eye your safe looks kinda flimsy. It ain't at all wise to tote around a fortune in jewels in a tin coffer like that."

"Cheques!" Gisèle said scornfully, ignoring everything else Joshua said. "But cheques must be taken to the banks to be changed into the *real* money. I do not take paper, M'sieur Joshua. Even your greenbacks I despise."

Edward Carter felt obliged to explain. "Mademoiselle Bourdette is paid always in gold coin . . . at the end of the first act. I must say it's laid down in the contracts every time."

"And the Eagles are stashed in this sardine can?" Joshua said incredulously.

"Comment?"

"Mr Dillard asks if the gold goes in the safe."

"Why, yes, Madame Guisard carries it back here while the performance continues and she counts it out. She brings it in this bag." Gisèle pulled out a battered chamois-leather bag tucked down behind the safe.

Joshua shook his head wonderingly. "Your Madame Guisard looked — uh — formidable in some ways. But I don't think her looks would scare off a backstreet mugger who'd gotten wind of what she carried in her bag."

Gisèle giggled, thinking of Marie Guisard's bulky figure, her mannish features and the dark, downy hair on her upper lip that might well repel some kinds of unwanted attention.

Joshua said sternly, "We're gonna have to do some serious talking about this, that's for sure." He turned to the impresario. "Hell, Carter, I don't cotton the set-up one bit."

Two black stewards brought in the crate of guns under the beady, watchful eyes of Madame Guisard.

Gisèle immediately diverted her attention to its opening. A contemptuous discussion of the nature of her coffers was both unfortunate and unnecessary as far as she was concerned. She had her self-esteem. Nor did she wish to quarrel with the interesting stranger. Far from it.

"Ah! Who would have thought a weapon could look so beautiful!" she exclaimed. She delved into the straw packing and produced a pearl-handled, silver-plated derringer.

"I must say Mr Maxwell told me he intended that this particular gun should be a personal gift to yourself," said Carter.

"I am charmed! Come, Henri, let us find you a fiercesome revolver!"

The hogleg produced for Henri did not improve his temper. He contemplated a reconditioned but clearly secondhand Remington, the peevish expression still set on his classical features.

"I accept this foolishness, Gisèle, but only to please yourself. It is enough that we have rehearsals and run-throughs to fill our hours, but now it seems there will be the target practice!" The disfiguring tic in the muscles of his even-featured face began bothering him again. It twitched spasmodically as he dared to question the wisdom of the woman who controlled his life.

"Henri, you must do it for me," she wheedled. "You have used a gun before and it will not be difficult. I know I can entrust you to see that the revolvers are distributed immediately to all the men in the company."

Rabier-Roget glowered, but he knew how to take a cue. The two stewards were summoned and he left, hostile yet, with the guns.

"Exit Henri Rabier-Roget — some annoyed," said Joshua. He tossed a box of cartridges he had kept back from the crate from hand to hand, then onto the shiny top of an upright piano, alongside the pistol Gisèle found so enchanting.

Carter took a watch from his vest pocket and flipped open the hinged cover. "I must say there will be no time for shooting games until we have left Argos City, Mr Dillard. We have a very tight schedule."

Joshua nodded. "But we gotta see to it Gisèle has that derringer properly loaded, and the sooner we can fix a trick or two for the defence of the stash of gold she's packing the better." He turned to the actress. "Have you a mind to palaver?"

Gisèle made a show of considering Joshua's request. "We must talk about it privately perhaps," she suggested, as though reluctant.

Joshua smiled, but inside, the woman sensed, he was still hard and grim. "Fine. Reckon the fewer folk who know what's planned, the safer it'll be for their own health and your money."

"That is right, Joshua. *Exactement*. I am glad we understand each other . . . You will excuse us, Marie, M'sieur Carter?"

Gisèle recognized something different and a little frightening about this man with the solemn, brooding expression. She had already admitted to herself she found him more than a little attractive. Of course, she laughed at his fears about her gold and Border badmen, but she would be more than happy to humour him if it was a way to get him alone, so that she had him all to herself to explore . . .

A long time had passed since a man had so excited Gisèle's interest. It was not simply Joshua Dillard's foreignness. It seemed as though he had built a chill wall around himself. She felt dared by the wall. A challenge was there. She was determined to climb the wall and fan into hot flame the fires she suspected she might find smouldering within.

6

The Trouble with Henri

JOSHUA DILLARD had broken open the cardboard box of .44 calibre cartridges and charged the derringer. He hefted the little Smith & Wesson gun, checking its balance and the feel of its decorative grips against his calloused palm.

"Have confidence in me, Joshua," Gisèle said, sidling up to him. "I have been on hunting expeditions and handled a Winchester."

"So you fancy yourself as a shot," Joshua replied, doubtfully. Women with an enthusiasm for guns were among the few things apt to make him feel nervous.

Gisèle gave him her tinkling laugh and placed a delicate hand on his sleeve. "Please! You are so melancholy, so serious. I believe you are sick at heart, Joshua, and you worry for nothing."

Joshua returned her a dry look. "I've not stayed to discuss my character," he said flatly. "This here is a meeting for plain business talk."

A moment of silence succeeded his cold words. Gisèle lowered her long-lashed eyelids and turned away.

"Forgive me. I go too far. It is Henri who has made you angry, of course. He is impossible! Even now he will be stoking his ridiculous jealousy with his disgusting morphine, plunging the needle through the cloth of his trousers, knowing it will upset me.

The revelation of Rabier-Roget's drug-taking did not surprise Joshua. His clean-cut looks were too good to be true. It had been hinted at by the newspaper critics that they covered up an inadequacy of acting talent. This was an area evidently in which he was deeply overshadowed by Gisèle. Perhaps he had been selected as a leading man with that intention. If so, small wonder he had turned to morphine.

"Why do you put up with the man?" Joshua asked bluntly.

Gisèle gave a Gallic shrug — a piece of ambiguous body language which somehow also managed to wriggle her hips kittenishly.

"Ah! You on your side of the ocean do not comprehend. You think desire is *abominable*. Henri is a very beautiful man, is he not? He is as strong as Hercules and his body is quite perfect."

Joshua was not shocked by the implications of what he thought Gisèle was trying to tell him. He was familiar with the concept so titillating to playgoers that the lovers they admired onstage were lovers offstage as well. But if Gisèle was merely serving such considerations, he felt an access of pity for her.

Memories of the short, cherished years with his beloved wife suddenly rushed in on Joshua with sharp poignancy.

"Well, Mademoiselle Bourdette," he said, "that sounds kind of sad to me."

"*Gisèle* . . . " the actress murmured correctingly. "And it is not right for you to grieve my position. I do not consider myself your American 'fallen woman'. *Non*. I have risen in the world. I belong to no one and am free, you understand? It is delightful to pick a leading man who is handsome and will worship me."

"Uh-huh," Joshua grunted. "It's your right, I guess." His tone was dismissive. All said and done, this was surely none of his business. Maybe Gisèle was just satisfying her reputed appetites, and as an abstract conventional morality wasn't something he set enough store by to argue for it.

But Gisèle saw no reason to change the topic.

"Of course, Henri can be absurd also. Sometimes he is as prudish as you Americans and the English. The teaching of his God-fearing mother — a countrywoman and a good Catholic — did not prepare him for the ways of Parisian society. He does not comprehend the protocol that goes with having an actress as a mistress."

Before he realized it, Joshua was fascinated into asking for explanation himself. "Can't say I'd figure that myself," he admitted. "You have special rules?"

"It is a tradition rather," she said, closing her eyes as she concentrated on choosing the right words. "The courtesan is accepted in my world, and she can have more than one lover. But one is her *amant de coeur*. She has chosen him and he has a hold on her heart and access to her bed when it is not otherwise occupied. Another might be a rich banker or high-ranking army officer who provides her with money and has first claim on her time."

"You mean you sell yourself to well-heeled old men." Joshua said distastefully.

Gisèle laughed. "You can see my

circumstances," she said, waving an airy hand at the luxurious surroundings. "I am independent now. That is to say, I can give my favours as I choose, which is to young artists rather than your old men! But it has not occurred to Henri that he should think of me as an *amant de coeur* would do. Where, alas, would he have learned the intrigues that are part and parcel of such adventures? He comes from a simple world where mothers and their teachings are sacred, women are submissive and sweethearts faithful."

"Is that so bad?"

"But yes! You see, for Henri to give a woman the gift of his body is not only a release and an explosive proof of his manliness. He must possess her exclusively. A woman who rejoices in being free to give herself elsewhere if she might decide so is unthinkable to him. He cannot respect her. He must raise her from the mire of sin and set her onto a pedestal of righteousness. In that he is a helpless puritan and a hypocrite. Because he is besotted and at heart he knows he is powerless, he turns for solace in morphine."

Joshua shook his head at this small speech. "Can't say's I rightly care for fandangle, Gisèle. Sounds to me like Henri has a plain case of jealousy."

Gisèle leapt on his words. *"Certainemnent!"* she said, a husky inflection to the French word. "He cannot countenance a rugged, capable man such as yourself engaging my interest."

"I wasn't referring to me in particular," Joshua demurred.

But she moved closer to him, smiling, a shameless vamp. She was, he had to concede, an exciting woman. And maybe an irresistible one . . .

She trailed her slim fingers on his sleeve and measured him frankly with her cat-like eyes. "I am so happy you are to travel with us, Joshua. You are a man who knows what has to be done, and can do it. You do like me, don't you? Men do, but so many are like silly boys. Or else they are petty and

91

small-minded, like Henri."

"Yeah," Joshua growled, meaning to put a stop to her play before it got *too* welcome. "There's small-minded folk everyplace — and for sure in end-of-the-tracks Texas cow towns. I saw off Argos City's hellfire preacher-man today. But you can bet silver cartwheels to pebbles there'll be other busybodies watching you, in this burg and every other like it. Folks in small towns make big talk out of nothing, I tell you."

"You are suggesting it will look bad if we were to spend some time together, is that not it?"

"You've got it in one, Gisèle!"

She appeared to muse, giving this her consideration.

"So! They will judge me by their imagining of what they are not here to see and the rumours they hear."

"It's more'n possible," Joshua said gruffly. "Gisèle, I think it's time I moved on out of here."

"*Pourquoi*? We already have the reputations, do we not? I am a brazen foreign hussy and you are a man who seizes his chances without conscience — a gun for hire. For why, then, must we deny ourselves what might be a pleasure?"

Her face was now only inches from his. She smiled up at him provocatively, exercising all her dangerous charms. She stood loosely, her small feet apart and visible beneath the hem of her gown, and her head thrown back, exposing the creamy white of her neck. The invitation was unmistakable.

Joshua was of flesh and blood, not stone. He was a man in his prime, a widower whose opportunities to satisfy his needs in ways acceptable to his own code were widely and unevenly spaced.

The temptation was beyond the bounds of endurance.

Why not? It wouldn't do any harm except to affront the morals of the prying stuffed shirts.

Suddenly, the time for pondering the question was gone. Raising herself on tiptoes, Gisèle flung her arms around his neck and kissed him firmly on his lips.

Joshua was used to being decisive, knowing what he wanted and acting accordingly. But this woman who was the product of an alien culture was a wonderment to him. He responded to her kiss, yet when they paused for breath, he asked, "Is this what you usually do with strangers?"

"No, but it is what I want to do with you," she said, unoffended. Then seemingly struck by the banal simplicity of her honest answer, she sighed and expanded on it in more reflective mood.

"The touring life is a whirlwind now that we have the steam engine in the place of the horse and wagon and the sail. The great artist no longer belongs to one country, nor even one continent. Time is so short for the personal things, Joshua, that sometimes we must ignore the ordinary formalities and cut the corners."

The reasoning emboldened and reassured him. He slipped off his coat. Assertively, and with a warm chuckle, he swept her off her feet and lifted her in his arms. Her surrendering body, as he'd expected, was light but incredibly supple. And he had no doubt about the effect it was having on him and his aroused masculinity.

"Gisèle, I'm going to take you at your word," he said, his voice hoarse with desire.

He swung around and went to lay her down on the plush cushions of an ottoman, but she squeezed his arm urgently. "Not here. Through the louvred doors you will find my sleeping quarters, and a bed wide enough for us to do all we wish."

Such explicit willingness dispersed any last vestige of restraint. Joshua shouldered his way into the inner compartment, glimpsing their unreal reflections in a gilded pier-glass and a carved mahogany dressing-table decorated with fresh, perfumed flowers.

They tumbled onto the embroidered covers of the bed, sinking into its softness. Gisèle giggled like a schoolgirl. She plucked at Joshua's shirt buttons and pressed her lips to his chest. An involuntary shudder went through her as she contacted the roughness of his hair.

Muscles spasmed beneath Joshua's rippling skin. No way could a man take this sweet torture passively. He fumbled with the fasteners and catches that imprisoned her within the shimmering blue gown, till impatient at his clumsy efforts Gisèle's own deft fingers intervened to achieve his goal for him. Her breasts, high and firm and with nipples fully erect, burst free from the close-fitting bodice.

"Quickly, Joshua, quickly!" she urged. "My passion admits no teasing, no subtlety!" Her breasts rose and fell with her erratic breathing.

Joshua peeled dress and shift down over her shapely white thighs. He swallowed as her underwear, too, was stripped away, revealing the glistening darkness of her pubic triangle. But her nakedness gave her no pause. Already her busy hands had tugged loose his belt and were working at the metal fasteners of his denims.

Her reckless wantonness inflamed him. Swiftly, he kicked out of pants and longjohns.

Garments flung aside, they reached for one another and entwined, limb to limb, torso to torso. They kissed hungrily. His erection probed demandingly against the tautness of her fluttering belly and she slipped one hand down to grasp and alleviate the awkward contact by guiding him between her parted legs. The intimate touch brought him to an aching hardness.

Their bellies rubbed together and Joshua slid his hands under her tight, smooth buttocks, gripping and lifting. She moved to help him, arching her slender pelvis, and he felt himself ease in between her swollen, pliant lips.

She moaned his name and he

abandoned the final vestige of control and thrust deeply into the yielding, slippery softness. She gasped and he felt her fingernails rake his shoulders. Then he was lost to everything bar the mounting, shared excitement in the rhythm of their movements, which became deeper and deeper until the woman beneath him was yelping with ecstatic pleasure.

He had never known a woman give herself so completely, so singlemindedly to the achievement of sexual gratification.

He strove to hold back, waiting for her, and it was this very solicitude that seemed to send her over some imaginary precipice, crying out fiercely and incoherently in her own language.

His own final release came instantly, with a pulsating, wild force that seemed to overpower his every sense. She went rigid beneath him, quite frighteningly breathless, then while she moaned, shaking her head from side to side, the sensation went on and on almost painfully till at last he was drained.

Minutes later they were still clinging together, the mingled sweat drying on their cooling bodies. Though utterly spent, Joshua felt a deep peace settling over him. They had accomplished a more complete satisfaction and contentment than he had believed such hasty coupling could ever produce.

Gisèle sighed dreamily, stroking his damp hair. "Joshua, *mon cher ami* . . . you are so strong, like a mountain lion. You have brought me to happiness and prostration, and I am exhilarated by it!"

He withdrew himself gently and rolled onto his back. "You were no disappointment to me either, Gisèle. The devil with your uncommon principles, I hope you'll feel no remorse later."

"Never!" She sat up with a jerk. "I do not find much happiness, Joshua. Always I seek the new sensation, the new emotions. That is how I will be until my life is worn away. If I had bypassed the Wild West and learned somehow it had cost me this afternoon, it is then I would have regrets!"

After this brief, passionate outburst, she began retrieving her hurriedly discarded clothing from among the rumpled blankets and Joshua reached for his pants. They sat on opposite edges of the wide bed, their backs to each other but dressing in a companionable, thoughtful silence.

Suddenly the calm was shattered.

The louvred door crashed back so hard against its stop, it bent and the brass knob struck the varnished wall panelling with a splintering crack.

7

Fist Fight in a Boudoir

HENRI Rabier-Roget sneered at the pair he had surprised *en deshabillé*. His disgust vied with his anger.

"Well, now," he said, misreading their dressing for undressing. "It seems I have arrived *just* in time to stop you making a mistake, Gisèle!"

He jerked his head at Joshua. "Get out of here, you dirty gunhawk, before I thrash you!"

Joshua climbed on to his feet. "You telling me what to do? That so, you're making a bigger mistake, friend!"

His tone was tart but he did nothing to point out that in the mistake stakes Rabier-Roget was already a length ahead, by jumping to a wrong conclusion. There would be no percentage in goading the unstable actor to a frenzy with the surprising truth that he had already bedded his mistress. Maybe Henri should have known better, but it was plain, and probably as well, he didn't credit Joshua — or more pertinently Gisèle — with being such a fast worker.

Nor did he read aright the situation that was developing now.

Rabier-Roget made no move to back off. Congestion darkened his too-handsome face, and the tic quivered in his left cheek.

"Get out, Dillard!" he demanded again. "You are contemptuous, saddle-tramp trash and you over-reach yourself by daring to enter Mademoiselle Bourdette's bedroom!"

"Henri!" Gisèle cut in. "Joshua is my invited guest. It is *you* who over-reaches himself!" Her remonstrance was like that of an interrupted mother stopping to plead with a truculent but tolerated child.

"Yeah, now you're making a helluva

mistake! Move your ass end outa here," Joshua said.

The actor chose to ignore or didn't hear the actress. When he saw Joshua, too, was standing his ground, daring to oppose him in this inner sanctum where he had supposed male rights to be exclusively his, he gave a smothered exclamation. "*Mon dieu*! I must throw you out!"

Rabier-Roget shot out a long arm and gripped Joshua's shoulder. Joshua felt his fingers like talons; the sharp fingernails punctured his bare skin. He was spun toward the open door.

The Frenchman was powerfully built, but the virility at which Gisèle had hinted was of a brash and aggressive kind. Even when Rabier-Roget tried to hold it down, his resonant voice boomed hollowly out of a chest that while broad was — Joshua suspected — also short of muscle and soft of fibre.

Joshua whirled back into the room. "Reckon you're dead set on locking horns with me at that!" he grunted. His right hand clenched into a fist which punched Rabier-Roget's belly like a piston.

The short, stabbing blow sank in and sent the breath whistling from the actor's mouth, opened as much by shock as the bruising impact.

"Messieurs!" Gisèle cried. "Stop! Let us be friends!"

Neither man took any notice.

Rabier-Roget staggered back, eyes boggling, but he recovered fast. "You damnable swine!" The worst damage was to his pride, and he went instinctively for swift reprisal. He lashed out with a looping right to Joshua's face.

Joshua rode the punch, back-pedalling out into the main salon. Even so, the actor's beringed knuckles grazed his jaw, tearing off skin. To counter with a hook of his own, he had to hit quickly while his enraged opponent was still coming forward under his own impetus.

He didn't like any part of this,

but he'd been purely pushed into retaliation.

Henri's even white teeth snapped together and he reeled away, gasping. The imprint of fury contorted his blond good looks. A trickle of red began and crept down slowly at the corner of his mouth.

Joshua's eyes were drawn by the first blood, which he thought would end the thing. That was maybe why he was caught out by Rabier-Roget's next move.

The actor dropped his head and his left hand went to his damaged mouth; his right to a coat pocket, reaching as Joshua thought for some kerchief. Too late, Joshua savvied the pocket's contents bulked too heavy and large for that.

When it reappeared Rabier-Roget's mitt was wrapped around the butt of the Remington revolver donated by Bennett Maxwell. Joshua was staring into the blue-black hole of its muzzle.

Rabier-Roget lifted the gun in a

white-knuckled, trembling hand. His forehead was beaded with sweat but a smile of grim triumph twisted his bloodied mouth.

Joshua saw the hammer lift under the tightening pressure of his trigger finger. The muzzle wavered unsteadily, yet at this range, in the suddenly tiny width of a railroad car, Joshua knew the odds were mighty slim that the emotional Henri could miss.

The tic went crazily in his cheek. He said, "I am going to kill you. Joshua Dillard!"

★ ★ ★

Miss Lorena Maxwell's day had turned sour. After the razzmatazz of the welcome for Gisèle Bourdette, Colby Vane had asked her to go buggy-riding with him.

Under her father's expectant eye, Lorena felt prevailed upon to accept the invitation. Still battered by the noise of the band and the crowd and fatigued by the mid-day heat, her wits had fumbled to come up with a justifiable excuse to refuse. Unsuccessfully.

"Sure, you younkers enjoy yourselfs," Bennett Maxwell said. "Me an' Gulliver'll step along to the club for some beers and a chin-wag."

Colby helped her mount to the single upholstered seat of the Vane surrey. His big hand fixed itself firmly under her elbow. Somehow her own hand, with which she'd gathered her long full skirts, got raised higher and higher by his insistent pressure. She noticed his hot eyes had simultaneously and equally become glued — on her exposed trim ankles and golden-skinned calves. She felt her cheeks burn.

Others, too, were looking on with keen interest. She glimpsed some winking and nudging among the nearer riffraff. By the sound of the knowing chortles, ribald remarks were exchanged.

It was infuriating. The last gossip she wanted spread around Argos City was that she was keeping company with Colby Vane!

Finally she was seated. But relief was short-lived. Colby dashed around the rig and fairly leaped up on the seat beside her. She thought he might land in her lap. He didn't, of course, but what did rapidly impress itself upon her as he took up the ribbons and put a fine pair of chestnuts into motion was that the seat was ridiculously small for two people. Especially if one meant to keep herself to herself.

The awareness of the lusty warmth of his body, penetrating their clothing where it pressed against hers at shoulder and thigh, disconcerted Lorena. She squirmed.

"Yeah, that's more like it. Git yuhself comf'table, Lorena," Colby said. He had a smugness about him. No doubt he was congratulating himself on the ease with which he had whisked her away from the hubbub — and from her obvious infatuation with the cultured New Yorker, Edward Carter.

This was just the way Colby Vane wanted it: the two of them alone. He was transparent. She could read his arrogant thoughts. *He* would soon bring her to her senses . . .

Well, just let him try!

They headed out of town, left the stage road and were soon on a minor trail through the B-Bar-M grass. The trail was less easy, but the springs of the surrey kept it running smoothly.

Nevertheless, that didn't stop Colby pitching himself against Lorena whenever the hint of a chance arose. Eventually, he got to draping a supposedly steadying arm around her shoulders.

Lorena tried to shrug his arm off, making it plain she wanted none of the intimacy he intended.

Colby finally figured he was getting the cold shoulder in spades. He applied some brake and tugged at the lines. One horse tossed her head and whinnied. Their progress slowed and the dust cloud churned up back of the surrey by the iron-rimmed wheels caught up and swirled around the pair on the seat.

"What's the matter, Lorena?" Colby burst out heatedly. "How come you're actin' up real unfriendly?"

Lorena sighed. There was no finesse about Colby Vane. In fact, he was plumb blunt. Maybe it was one of his good points. However, that was no consolation to a girl in her predicament.

"I don't think it would be very smart of me to do anything to encourage you," she said. She picked the words carefully, aware of how easy it would be to fall into the same trap of bluntness. As she made it, her comment directed anything that might sound like criticism to herself.

"Hell! What's that s'posed to mean?"

"Colby, whatever you may think, I don't see you as my beau. Your — your shining up to me is apt to get tiresome."

The last bit came from Lorena's trembling lips in a rush.

Colby chewed it over, his ponderous

jaw working silently, his sandy brows lowered.

"Huh!" he scoffed at last. "I know what it is. Reckon yuh've got the hots for that New York cissy!"

His crudeness didn't shock her. It was at one with his solid, forthright, hard-muscled ways. Nor did she let his accusation rile her, though she was put out to learn it was visible to others that she was attracted by Edward Carter.

"It isn't that at all!" she protested, no matter she knew it was a partial lie. "We may have both grown up as kids on this range, but that doesn't mean our paths will always be the same. Indeed, it means *nothing*."

She gestured at the familiar landscape around them, the shrubs of semi-desert, creosote bush, ocotillo and mesquite, giving way to prairie. "You belong here, Colby — in this wilderness — whereas deep in my soul I know I do not."

A breeze from the west had sprung up while they'd been riding. She'd not noticed it before they'd slowed, but she told herself absently it must be its dampish touch bringing her a sudden shiver.

Colby sniggered. "That's rich, comm' from the daughter o' the richest cattleman in the county!"

His remark was gallingly perceptive. Lorena felt guilty at her disloyalty to the country and the way of life that had given her sustenance.

"Try as hard as I might, I find nothing to admire in this rough and savage world," she defended herself. At least explaining her own motives was preferable to expressing her opinions of the person and personality of Colby Vane, which would be liable to further bruise his bullish dignity.

"There is a veneer of civilization in my father's houses and in the opera house he has built," she went on. "But it's not enough. I hate the 'necessary' cruelty involved in the stockman's business, however humane its practice."

"Shucks . . . "

"Our system is pure terrorism, from the time the calf is forced into the branding-chute and the hot iron sears his cringing flesh until the day he is driven from his free graze and crammed in a railroad car to be shipped to the Eastern slaughterhouses. It disgusts me and I want to be free of it."

Colby sneered. Heeling calves, herding them to corral or chute for branding, the round-ups and the drives of cattle to railyards, were fun and frolic in his way of thinking. The only reality he could comprehend was the one he knew and treasured in ranch life.

"The hell with purty speeches! Would it be so bad a thing gittin' hitched to me, Lorena?"

Lordsakes! Was this some kind of marriage proposal, Lorena wondered. With his metaphor the boy made it sound like something you did with a horse and wagon. He might be the son of the president of the Stock Association, but he talked and

113

acted like an oafish cowpuncher. She shuddered.

"I don't think you've understood a word I've said!" she exclaimed. "Must I go on? I don't want to spend my life here. I want to quit this land. I need to travel far, not to someplace over the next hill or across the next river."

"Yuh ain't talkin' sense, Lorena. Lissen good. Yore pa won't let yuh pull out. He ain't got no son to step inta his boots when he hangs up his hat fer keeps. Yuh gotta marry him a good man!"

Colby nodded his square head, as he considered and confirmed the logic of his argument. The wisdom of his twentysome years, and his own pa's hints, told him he was the hombre old man Maxwell was looking to.

Lorena could see Colby was still implying that she was destined to be his bride, but she didn't even want to discuss their futures on such a dangerously personal level.

She waved her hand at the terrain

again, noticing at the same time clouds had been gathering over it as they argued, casting shifting shadows over the wind-stirred crop of grama grass. The cooling westerly had a wetness to it.

"The range-cattle industry is a way of life that can't last for ever," she predicted. "There's no sense in folk ordering their lives according to a bygone boom that made their fathers' fortunes. Maybe one day the land will quit *them*."

"That's stinkin' thinkin'," Colby growled. He could no way envisage a time when the joyous whoop of the puncher would no longer be heard across this land.

Colby, too, suddenly awoke to the realization that for the time of day it had grown uncommon gloomy. He looked up at the massing of black clouds directly above them. He turned his dry-skinned, sun-hardened face to the wind and sniffed. Rain was in the offing, that was certain sure.

"Damn the luck!" he cussed. "It's gonna rain an' we ain't got no slickers."

"We'll never get back to town or the B-Bar-M before it reaches here!" Lorena complained.

"Tell yuh what — we c'n git as far as Arnott's old ranch-house."

"That old sieve of a shack!" Lorena cried. Arnott had been one of the pioneers whose spread had been absorbed into her father's holdings and its adobe and lumber buildings had been allowed to fall into gradual decay.

"Better'n nothin'," Colby said.

Lorena looked briefly at the threatening sky. "Well, have it your own way then, but the roof's full of holes." Her voice was loaded with scepticism.

Colby smirked. Sure he was going to have it his own way. This sudden rainstorm could be a blessing. He hoped it might last an hour or two.

It had quickly occurred to him that once they were out of the surrey and he had Lorena bailed up in the Arnott place, he could

116

get his hands on her properly and there'd be nothing stopping him from teaching the uppity wench to be more damned civil.

He licked his dry lips and felt his pulses quicken as he imagined the ways he might make it a lesson she couldn't ignore or forget. He knew how to deal with reluctance. Hell, he'd broken in scores of mettlesome mockies, hadn't he? He'd put on the cack and screw it down.

With a crack of the whip, Colby broke the chestnut pair into a hell-for-leather run toward a mile-distant ridge. In its lee lay the abandoned homestead.

A flicker of lightning lit the undersides of the black clouds and the skyline of the distant rim to their left. Moments later came the low grumble of thunder. Big drops of rain started to fall, settling the dust and making dark splatters on a rocky, disused trail.

Lorena was bounced on the surrey's seat cushions and she clung to the side of the coachwork. Not all her apprehension had to do with the coming storm and the hectic ride. Colby's eagerness added distrust to her unhappy feelings.

8

Close Call

JOSHUA DILLARD froze like a cornered jack-rabbit. The cocked hammer had only to fall on the loaded chamber of the Remington revolver gripped by Henri Rabier-Roget to produce the flaming, ear-splitting blast of an exploding shell. The heavy slug would rip into his flesh with a jarring slam. Gut-shot, twisted with pain, his body would fold forward and crumple and he would be a half-naked, lifeless heap in Gisèle Bourdette's *de luxe* railroad car.

Joshua stared down the long, nickelled barrel at imminent death.

He wiped his mouth with the back of his hand as though the sharp tang of cordite smoke was already in it and he was trying to get rid of the bitter taste of defeat and annihilation.

It was a moment of truth and fleeting, final analysis in which he cursed himself for all kinds of a fool. Once there'd been sense and order in his life, back when he'd been an operative with the renowned Pinkerton Detective Agency.

But he had few regrets about the severing of those ties. Nor did he much care to roam the haunted corridors of memory; they always led back to San Antonio, Texas, where the light of his younger life — his beautiful, blue-eyed, golden-haired wife — had been ruthlessly blown away by the aggrieved Wilder outlaw gang, precipitating his resignation as a Pinkerton.

He'd never really come to terms with his loss. His love dead, a part of him had been torn out and thrown away, leaving emptiness, an ache that plagued him constantly.

Therein, too, lay the roots of his obsession: to hunt down all lawbreakers, brace them, kill them. The obsession was forever present like a grim shadow that could never be cut loose as he worked as a freelance agent. Often, the personal mission of death-dealing undermined good judgment, distracting him from a job at hand. Always, it seemed to keep him poor, careful though he was as a soldier of fortune and professional fighting man to hire out his gun only at the right price.

Short-term get-rich schemes like becoming an adviser to a touring theatre troupe therefore had to be irresistible.

Maybe his problem was he couldn't keep off the sidetrails that led to trouble. With the distractions of risk and adventure, rationalized by the requirements of a broad vengeance, he didn't have time to question how he led his blighted life.

Yet his present predicament wasn't exactly like that. It was plain stupid. He should have known better than to he drawn into this mess he was in with an over-sexed French actress, searching for new diversions, and her jealous lover.

Every step of the rushed and rash way to Gisèle's bed, he had surely asked for it.

Now it was too late for self-recrimination. Rabier-Roget's gun was up and levelling. It was about to bang and buck in the Frenchman's hand . . .

Thunk!

Chunks of metal came together, but nothing else happened.

Rabier-Roget glared at the shooting-iron in his fist, his face a comic mask of surprise. He triggered again. The same grinding result turned his look to frustration, then anger.

"Sacristi! C'est defectueux," he snarled, and hurled the useless weapon at Joshua's face.

Joshua caught the bruising missile on his raised right forearm. He was numbed from fingertips to elbow, but it was nothing to a bullet in the chest.

"Henri!" Gisèle begged. "We must talk this over!"

But the jamming of the gun's

mechanism had made Rabier-Roget look foolish on top of his other grievances. His pride was already badly hurt. He threw himself after the jammed Remington, fists again swinging.

Joshua gave ground till he backed into the upright piano. Trapped, he slammed a hard and accurate punch, left-handed, at the point of the actor's chin.

Rabier-Roget went staggering back, tangling his heels in what looked like a zebra-skin rug and upsetting a potted palm. With a bellow of pain, he sat down heavily on his backside. But he was soon back on his feet and he grabbed up a small rosewood table. He advanced on Joshua, thrusting its curved legs at Joshua with a stabbing motion.

Joshua seized the legs, twisted and wrenched the table from Rabier-Roget's grasp.

Gisèle screamed. *"Assez!"* She looked around at the magnificent fittings — the brass lamps, the stained glass, the playwrights' busts and the china figurines — and feared she would see the regal splendour of her special Pullman car smashed to smithereens about her. "I order you to stop this!"

Her words fell on deaf ears.

Joshua swept the table low at Rabier-Roget's legs. The enraged actor gave another howl, but stumbled and trampled right over it, breaking it into splintered pieces.

In desperation, Gisèle rushed across the parlour and caught up the pearl-handled derringer from where it had been left, loaded, on the shiny black top of the cold wood stove. She had a shrewd idea the stubby-barrelled gun would punch its .44 calibre slugs clear through the Pullman's roof. But it was a situation that called for stern measures. Least, it might startle the men to their senses and hold off a total wreck.

She raised the small gun above her head in her right hand and braced her wrist with her left. She squeezed the trigger.

Click!

Like the Remington, it failed to fire and Joshua and his attacker kept on slugging away at one another regardless, though Joshua had seen what Gisèle was up to from the corner of one shocked eye.

Joshua tripped on a remnant of the table and Rabier-Roget landed a near rabbit punch on the back of his neck. Joshua's vision blurred and his ears sang, but somehow he managed to keep his wits as he fell.

Rabier-Roget swung a booted foot at his head.

Cat-like, Joshua rolled clear of the wicked kick. The fight was getting dirty, but his reactions were trained to meet the worst. He'd learned his rough-house stuff in a hard school and learned it well.

He scrambled to his feet, gasping. "Looks like I'm gonna have to take you to pieces, skunk," he said.

★ ★ ★

Marie Guisard heard men's voices raised in anger and the sounds of fighting. Her heart hammered within her stout chest. Her fears were not for the men but for Gisèle Bourdette — for whom she cared as though she were a daughter — and for the safety and good of the company.

She didn't like these primitive frontier towns that so fascinated Gisèle. It would have been better, she considered, if they'd been left off the itinerary for the *grand voyage*. The dowdy womenfolk were submissive and coarsened by hard work and their harsh surroundings. The best of the menfolk were gentlemanly enough, but they were also aggressive and arrogant; tall and tough, loud and proud . . .

The gunman Joshua Dillard, whom she knew had caught Gisèle's eye, was all the more dangerous because she sensed he was something apart from the typical stock. Grim experience was

126

etched in the lines of his face and she sensed no man could be his master, or his mistress. They said his dubious talents were freely available for money, but her intuitive reading of him told her he would stick first and last to his own code and serve his own — to her — mysterious ends.

Madame Guisard was accustomed to Gisèle behaving outrageously. Indeed, the actress could be said to have led a life resembling that of the improbable Feuillart and Dumas heroines she played on stage. Her amazing wilfulness and individuality were, Madame Guisard believed, what had alienated influential parts of the Parisian theatrical establishment and were behind the establishment of Gisèle's own company and embarkation on the extensive American tour.

But this time, with Joshua Dillard, Gisèle was playing with fire.

The more so because her current leading man and therefore lover, the provincially-minded Henri Rabier-Roget, had as much pride as any of the

Texans and was anxious to impose his standards on Gisèle, all be they double ones.

Her hirsute lips trembling, Madame Guisard mouthed a silent prayer in the next railroad car and tried to mind her own business, at which she was very practised and good.

When the thumps gave way to crashes and Gisèle screamed, she knew the time had come to act.

She rushed from her private berth to summon help. Some other men of the company must be prevailed upon to intervene.

But none was to be found.

"Where are they?" she asked a young artiste, reclining with a piece of damp flannel draped over her brow.

The woman moaned. "They went into the town, madame, to a restaurant. Their stomachs are sick of sandwiches and preserves and tins of sardines. Me, I am sick of head, of their games noisy and ceaseless of baccarat and piquet. and I must rest for the performance."

The run of the company did not have access to Gisèle's more lavish quarters, which included a private dining-room in which two black cooks, working from an adjoining galley, were contracted to present the wonders of American cuisine.

Madame Guisard tutted her dismay. Hot though it still was outside despite gathering black clouds, she pulled on a sealskin ulster that was a gift from Gisèle. Without stopping to belt it, she lumbered off in search of the absent players.

She pounded down a cinder path, flanked by the pole fences of smelly cattle pens, which led toward the ugly rears of the erections that flanked the main street. She could not think of them as buildings; only the dominating opera house deserved this appellation.

In the end, Madame Guisard did not locate the restaurant and the underprivileged French diners. She met instead Edward Carter Jnr, Bennett Maxwell and Gulliver Vane leaving the cattlemen's club back of a sprawling establishment proclaimed by an ornate sign to be the Paradise Saloon — Bill Baker, Prop. In actual fact, the place was heavily mortgaged to a real estate company chaired by Maxwell.

She saw three capable men, two of them solidly built, and breathlessly poured out her story.

The men held their tongues until she'd finished. They were impressed by the whiteness of her shocked face and had to strain to follow her gabble, delivered in broken English.

"By God!" Maxwell blurted indignantly. "That hellion Dillard'll leave a fancy French actor like ground beef! We gotta stop the crazy sonofabitch!"

Carter was first to take to his heels for the railroad depot. "It's apt to sound like the Chief has given me a bum steer this time! Which isn't like him at all . . . "

Vane took Madame Guisard's arm and followed less precipitately in the wake of his erstwhile drinking pards.

Desperation was in the old French-woman's voice. "That poor Monsieur Rabier-Roget!" she wailed to Vane. "I fear he will be not remain in a condition to tread the boards at the opera house!" She had no great liking for Henri but she recognized his importance to the company's performances.

Her fears were also heightened by superstition. "I have told Mademoiselle Bourdette it is not right for us to arrive in the bright sunlight," she said. "It is a very bad omen for what is an opening night in your town."

But when she reached Gisèle's Palace car, she was cheered to see Carter and Maxwell had respectively dragged apart Dillard and Rabier-Roget.

Gisèle had interposed her small but dominating presence between them, her feet planted in the crumple of a Persian hanging torn from a wall.

The car was a shambles. Furbelows were scattered all over. Potted plants were overturned, flowers crushed. A *chaise longue* sagged, its framework

131

snapped in the middle. Split satin cushions off a divan spilled feather stuffing.

Rabier-Roget exhaled gustily, the breath whistling through his loosened teeth and his cut and bloody lips.

"I demand the dismissal of this scoundrel, Gisèle! I wish to see an officer of the American law, Monsieur Maxwell!"

Gisèle closed her eyes briefly. "Henri, you could have killed Monsieur Dillard with your pistol. Now the fighting has stopped, will it not be better if we make peace and try to forget this stupidity?"

"Yeah." Joshua clipped. "You had no right pulling a hogleg on me, big boy."

Rabier-Roget began to bristle anew and Maxwell tightened his grip on his arm.

Carter said, "Drop it, Mr Dillard. Mademoiselle Bourdette and Argos City need this man in one piece, tonight!"

The young impresario was as single-minded as ever in his determination to keep the wheels of the theatrical tour turning smoothly. It might not be this way in the long run, but for the moment he saw the company's gunhand as a fly in the ointment.

He pulled Joshua aside. "Monsieur Rabier-Roget is all riled up," he went on quietly.

"No question about that," Joshua said, tight-lipped.

"There's a misunderstanding here, and it may take quite a bit of talking to straighten out. I must say the best scheme would be for you to lie low — leastways, till the Argos City performance is over and we're ready to ride the rails again."

Joshua didn't see things from the same perspective. He might have hired out his services, but this had gotten kind of personal and he was a man whose basic instinct was to do as he was minded. "I ain't the type to put my tail 'tween my legs and skulk in shadows," he rasped.

"Now don't get sore, Mr Dillard! Listen here, the point is — ."

"Stick your blasted point!" Joshua shot back tersely. "The fight is the gink's and mine, and I didn't come hunting no trouble. He was gonna throw down on me, and that's a goddamned fact. I'm a tolerant man, Mr Carter, but not with fools on the prod. You'd better start thinking about a replacement if'n you want some tame wet-nurse for this bunch of crackpots! 'Cause I'm quitting, as of now!"

"Mr Dillard, don't be foolish! Mademoiselle Bourdette's tour is the event of the American theatrical decade. You have a contract and I must say my father is agreeable to paying you a large share of the profits. Stay with us. Do what you have to do . . . "

Joshua shrugged. "That don't cut no ice with me. Maybe there's things more important than a thick bankroll. Maybe there's self-respect."

Carter gulped disbelievingly. "You can't walk out on us!"

"Can. And just have. The hell with Gisèle, Rabier-Roget, Maxwell and the whole damn boiling!"

9

'You Can't Do This!'

THE old Arnott ranch-house was in as bad a state of repair as Lorena Maxwell had remembered. The rain drummed down on it noisily, a full-fledged cloudburst, blowing in through the glassless apertures that had been windows and pouring in splashy torrents through the countless holes over their heads.

"What a dump!" Lorena said, screwing up her normally straight and pretty nose.

Colby Vane laughed in a high-pitched way. "It'll serve jest fine. Thar's shingles enough still on the roof to make some dry spots. Set yuhself down, willya?"

He yanked her down beside him onto the malodorous, faded red blanket covering a mattress on a creaking bunk. She shuddered.

"Yeah, gettin' cold, ain't it?" he said in a paradoxically satisfied way. "But I guess I know how I c'n keep us warm!" He laughed again, put his arm around her waist, pulled her close.

Colby was remembering how his father had said it would be a fine thing if he was to start to courting the Maxwell gal good and proper, and he was nothing loath. No siree!

Lorena felt his curiously heavy breath hot on her cheek and recoiled from him in distaste. She turned her face to the split-log wall and studied the flaking clay that plugged the joints.

Colby knew when he was getting the brush-off. "Aw, c'mon, honey!" he said abruptly, impatiently. "Loosen up! I'd like to kiss you. It's nice 'n' private. What's wrong with a kiss — one kiss?"

For a would-be Romeo Colby Vane was too uncouth and rough ever to succeed in arousing Lorena's interest.

Now push had come to shove, she was going to have to tell him.

"You mustn't talk like that, Colby," she said, striving to keep her nervous voice level. "You mustn't *feel* like that."

"Why not?" he asked, incredulous. "Thar's nothin' wrong with kissin' me, Lorena. Hell, I've kissed lots o' gals."

"I'm sure that's true," Lorena prevaricated. "An' they enjoyed it," he added stridently. "But I'm afraid I'm not like those other girls, Colby. What you might have done with them doesn't prove anything. I told you, I have no sentimental feeling about you. I don't even admire any of the things in life that you do."

"God almighty! Don't start that up ag'in!" Being reminded of the words they'd exchanged in the surrey also reminded Colby that he was no longer handicapped by having to control the rig and its team, and that he'd resolved to put this advantage, once achieved, to practical use.

Moreover, he wasn't going to have it whispered back to the Argos City populace that any female, however high-and-mighty, could play a Vane along for a sucker. He started feeling real mean.

And the girl's slim, stiffened figure kept right on intoxicating his inflamed desires.

"Yuh're gonna kiss me, damnit!" he said. "Whether yuh like it or not, whether yuh feel anythin' or not!"

"Kissing me isn't going to help any, you or m — "

Colby pressed his mouth on hers in a hard, wet, demanding kiss, and the words were stifled in Lorena's arched throat as she tried to pull away.

But he had a horny hand clapped at her nape and the best she could do was allow herself to go utterly lax and keep her mouth shut and her own stilled lips carefully unresponsive.

Colby worked at them bruisingly. She moaned in protest. All that moved him to do was shift his hand, it seemed, dislodging her hair pins, so the shiny black tresses tumbled about their faces and to her shoulders.

Lorena went to pull away then, not realizing that Colby's hand had gone no farther than to the hooks and buttons at the back of her dress. When she pulled, the fastenings he was fiddling with parted and the top of her dress slid from her shoulder.

Colby yanked at fine fabric and lace and suddenly her bodice was ripped open, baring the warm-gold orb of one breast to his feverish gaze.

He clutched at her; she felt his palm clammy against the sensitive bud of a nipple made erect by the sudden, shocking exposure to the cool of the storm-broken air.

"You can't do this!" Lorena screamed. She struck him a cracking blow across the face with an open hand and leaped up, pulling the dress back onto her shoulder.

Red marks showed on Colby's visage where her fingers had hit and the nails trailed. Her own hand stung from the force of the slap and the abrasive contact with the bristles on his shaven cheek.

The frenzy in her left Colby, who'd been mesmerised by the uncovered charms of her body, momentarily flummoxed. Then he got to his feet, glaring at her murderously, and came after her, his fists balled like hard rocks.

"Why, you little hellcat!" he said through gritted teeth.

Lorena might have had a preference for the gentler, cultured side of life, but she'd grown up in a tough environment and was no milksop. She knew attack was sometimes the best kind of defence. Before Colby could decide whether he was to hit out at a woman or master his raging temper, she ran at him and gave him a mighty shove in the chest.

Colby tottered on the high heels of his boots. They were thirty-dollar Justins of the riding kind made to fit a stirrup. He reeled back — straight under the biggest stream of stormwater cascading through the leaky roof.

He roared. In truth, he was a physical young man. Lorena's words, which should have been like a dash of cold water to his passions, had been ineffective. But a dousing in the real stuff produced exactly the right result.

He spluttered and shook himself like a hosed dog. Lorena said, "You'll keep your paws off me, or so help me, I'll — I'll — " She didn't really know, but fortunately it no longer mattered.

"Awright, Miss Lorena Maxwell, I hear yuh! I'm wet through. One helluva note, lemme tell yuh." He started squeezing water from the sleeves and cuffs of his Sunday-best suit coat.

"When it stops raining, which is beginning to sound like soon, you'll take me back to town with no more hanky-panky," Lorena ordered.

"Shore!" he said. "But no never mind, Lorena, I'll get what I want — yuh'll see."

"How do you mean?"

"Yuh must know how it is! My pa's expectin' me an' you to — uh — get acquainted real close." He paused and, fearing he might not have made himself plain, added, "Man t' woman."

"No disrespect. but fiddlesticks to your father!"

"I don't know 'bout that. I jest so happen to hear yore pa likewise's expectin' yuh to shine up to me." He laughed humourlessly. "Guess yuh gonna have to toe the line some day, li'le lady!"

★ ★ ★

Joshua Dillard walked the narrow strip of polished floor between the truckle bed and the chintz-curtained window of his attic room with its view of the incongruously Doric frontage of the opera house.

For a while after he'd stormed out of Gisèle Bourdette's Palace car, his anger had burned. But a couple of bottles of the beer he'd brought back to the boarding house had dampened the fires somewhat. Regret at the loss of attractive business and a disgust with himself was starting to creep up on him.

Apart from the money side of it, he hated unfinished business. He'd no stomach for deferring to a French actor inspired by jealousy and possibly morphine, but maybe he was doing exactly what he'd said he wouldn't — tucking his tail between his legs and running.

And to put the mildest construction on it, Gisèle Bourdette had aroused his interest. Their moments together had been damned good as well as surprising, he reminded himself with bitter reproach at the loss of their potential repetition. But why should he be surprised? The famous actress was by nature still a courtesan, wasn't she? A French whore, according to those legions of his fellow American citizens who found her antics offensive.

Hell, he was no puritan but he'd

found her free indulgence in the pleasures of the flesh hard to come to terms with himself.

Yet he knew it wasn't only that but something else niggling at the dark back corners of his mind. He tried to drag it into the light.

In the steadily dimming confines of the small, stuffy room, he failed, and found himself again at the window.

His gaze sharpened. A cloudburst earlier had passed over, the slanting downpour driven on from Argos City by a persistent wind. Down in the laid dust of the clean-smelling streets, hawkers were selling cribs containing a rough translation of the French play being put on at the opera house. Tickets, too, were changing hands at fancy prices.

Dusk had come and opera house patrons were arriving outside the imposing edifice. In the yellow glow of its lamps, they gathered and strutted like courting prairie chickens on a lek, preening themselves in their finery, flapping and consulting their cribs.

Joshua had been offered one of the cribs himself on his way back to his room. It had looked adequate enough to give an audience the drift of the action, but he suspected that with few folks in Argos City being fluent in French, the company would be able to take liberties with the text as they chose. The attractions for the Texans would be other than niceties of language. It would be spectacle — the wonderful costumes and draperies — and the stunning Gisèle Bourdette in daring scenes with her reputed lover, Henri Rabier-Roget.

Beauty and titillation would brighten their mundane lives in exchange for their wearisomely earned dollars.

The chink of coin and rustle of bills from below crystallized Joshua Dillard's concerns. Bourdette's company was to be paid, by her quaint whim, in gold coin at the playhouse, at the end of the first act. Edward Carter Snr had written him in Mexico that Gisèle's average earnings per performance in the United States were running at 20,000 francs. He didn't know how many American Double Eagles that would amount to, but it sounded a hell of a lot of loot in any currency.

He checked himself. It was none of his business anymore. "You keep outa this, Joshua m' boy," he told himself. "It ain't got nothing to do with you."

But there were lawless elements in this country, and big money like this would draw them like flies to a moist sugarplum. That's why he'd insisted on arming the troupe.

The guns!

Suddenly Joshua knew what it was gnawing away at the edges of his brain. He swore under his breath at the way events had distracted him. dulling his wits. "Former detective!" he derided in self-contempt.

Two guns had been drawn and triggered in Gisèle's rolling parlour. Neither had fired. Did Joshua believe coincidences like that ever really happened? Or did they have to be set up?

Joshua grunted a no to the first question, which meant a yes to the second. In short, he quickly concluded the guns had been tampered with to ensure they both jammed!

He got to wondering about the state of the rest of the revolvers that had been handed out to the theatrical party. Due to his resignation, he had no idea what level of protection or defence there would be against a determined raid on Maxwell's theatre. Even now a huge and tempting sum of money was being amassed at the opera house for changing into the gold coin that apparently would be collected by Madame Marie Guisard during the course of the performance, in compliance with the French company's custom and contract.

Joshua chewed his lip irritably. The idea that dirty work was afoot, with the money as its stimulus, drew him like a fish to a baited hook.

Thief-taking was more than a business to him. It was a way of life; a means of making sense of his imperfect present by imbuing himself with motives that sprang from the grief of the past. Every time he went up against badmen, he chased a tantalizing shadow of redress for the deep and still-hurting scars inflicted by outlawry.

It was why he couldn't hang up his gun — and why now he gave some thought to going to Edward Carter Jnr and withdrawing his resignation.

"Like hell I will!" he soliloquized through gritted teeth. "There's no damned way I could work with that lousy outfit, so I might as well forget about it."

He let himself drop onto the creaking truckle bed, tugged off his boots and opened another bottle.

10

Loco Louey Comes to Town

THE opera house was not the only show in town. For some there was nothing to beat cockfighting — not even the exotic allure of a dazzling French actress of high acclaim and scandalous reputation.

To the cockpit that night came Luis Velarde. It said much about the policing of Argos City, and Loco Louey's disregard for it, that though he came deviously and without fanfair, he did nothing much to conceal his identity.

Velarde found the fetid indoor enclosure in the town's ramshackle Mexican quarter packed shoulder to shoulder with heated bodies surrounding the closely supervised fighting pit. It was a family occasion, too. The crowd numbered men and women both, of all ages, even children.

In his homeland, south of the Border, cockfighting was the diversion of the people, not the Latin aristocrats, and Velarde was always pleased to be seen congregating with the fowl fanciers, placing his bets with the gamesters, rubbing shoulders with the cockers who pitted their birds to the death in the prize ring.

Acceptance by such company boosted his image as champion of the *peons* — not a brigand but a rebel. That he oppressed the poor people himself, exploiting them and slowly destroying them with his drug and prostitution rackets, was a matter he never dwelled on.

"Ocho a cinco!" he cried. "Eight to five on the black!" He pulled sweat-stained bills from the shirt that strained over his big belly and waved them above his head. Somebody took the bet, and he settled down to watch the fight, plucking at the tips of his black moustachios.

"Pit!" the stern call was given.

The cockers instantly turned the gamebirds loose and the bout began. A prize red rooster, who tipped the scales at a heavy five and one fourth pounds, confronted the black contender that was Velarde's own pick.

The birds' ruffs bristled. Hatred and the inbred lust to rule the roost gleamed in their bright beady eyes. These creatures needed no encouragement to do battle. They went at one another beak and claw.

Velarde was no deep thinker, but as diversions went there was nothing in his book to rival the excitement of the cockfight. He licked his fat wet lips and his protuberant eyes shone. It was the kill, of course; the swift disposal of the losers and the weak. A knockout in this ring was unfailingly accompanied by blood and extinction. So eminently satisfactory. So conclusive.

It was how life and death should be.

Both roosters wore Mexican gaffs on

their spurs. Velarde was fascinated by the glinting, double-edged, razor-keen blades. They were quite wicked and lethal, being nearly three inches long. They could easily slash the throat of an adversary, poke out an eye or amputate a comb.

A small brown-skinned boy at his elbow yelled shrilly, *"Picale en el corazon!"* Stick him in the heart . . . Velarde admired the youngster's zest.

The cocks, with combs erect, tore at one another with beaks sharp as pointed scissors. Soon, blood flowed freely from their wounds.

Velarde cussed when he saw the black getting the worst of it, his feathers matted with vivid red gore around the head and neck.

The black's owner shook like a leaf. "I am very sorry, *Señor* Velarde. The red is much fierce. It looks like you will lose your stake. I make apology."

"*Amigo*, the test is not yet over. He is not dead. You will patch him up between rounds."

The cocker made every effort to carry out the outlaw chief's order. He tended the cut and ripped flesh as best he could. He pursed his lips and blew mightily, targeting hot, moist breath on the feathers above the bird's rump. Attention to this vital area was said to stimulate the cock's whole bloodstream.

"Pit!"

Velarde watched avidly as the black, partially restored by his owner's ministrations, returned to the fray with quickened belligerence.

But the big red stood his ground, a veteran of the mains, waiting his chance to vanquish his less experienced foe. It came midway through the pitting. Velarde sighed as the red felled the black with a vicious kick and sank the point of his gaff deep into the battered adversary's head.

Blood spurted from the gaping hole.

The black writhed in the dust, fluttering his once-gleaming, broken plumage spasmodically and awkwardly threshing his feet about so the gaffed spurs sliced at air and his own pinions.

Velarde shook his head and sighed again, and his fancied bird died.

The red puffed up his bruised chest with the tainted air, digging his bloodied talons into the packed dirt. Exhausted though he was, he produced a taunting crow of victory.

Velarde shoved a wad of greenbacks at the man who'd accepted his wager. He smiled greasily, insincerely. "Your bet, *señor. Gracias.*"

The transaction completed, Velarde turned away, his features immediately taking on a grouchy cast that reflected his true feelings. Maybe he should arrange for a lesson to be taught the dead cock's owner . . . A fire at his hennery perhaps, to wipe out his breeding stock.

A nondescript Mexican chose this moment to sidle up to him. His face was sallow and thin under the broad brim of a sombrero; his feet were bare, one limping leg was wasted and his flimsy cotton trousers threadbare and ragged at the bottoms.

But Velarde said nothing. He recognized the pathetic wreck as the menial who usually did chores in the cookhouse for the rich gringo of the B-Bar-M ranch. The man thrust a sealed envelope into his hand and he scantly nodded his thanks.

Under a hissing lamp, Velarde put aside his thoughts of punishment for the cocker. He ripped open the envelope and unfolded the single, closely-written sheet inside.

The reading of it brought a slackening of the taut muscles in his grim face. But the beginnings of an avaricious smile made him look no less ugly.

What was it to lose a few measly dollars on a cockfight?

His smile broadened. Soon, he was going to be loaded with gold pieces. The money was his for the taking at Bennett Maxwell's opera house. Here were the final details all neatly spelled out.

Bueno! It was all better than he'd dared anticipate.

Even the range-dick gunman Joshua Dillard could be removed from his calculations, it seemed, despite the failure of Mendoza and his band to eliminate him previously. And the men of the foreign acting company were all carrying weapons that would prove useless!

Velarde screwed up the paper, stuffed it in his pocket and rubbed his hands together. With inside knowledge like this, he couldn't fail. He was about to pull off the biggest caper of his life. A fortune would be his and maybe he wouldn't have to fire a shot.

But he'd play it double-safe. Lighting a short brown cigarette, he left the cockfight and went to collect the two trusted *compadres* who'd accompanied him to town.

★ ★ ★

Lorena Maxwell was curiously unaffected as Gisèle Bourdette sinned and suffered as Marguerite Gautier in the Dumas *fils* play *La Dame aux Camélias*. Nor did the broad-shouldered, lean-loined masculinity of Henri Rabier-Roget, who played opposite the star as her lover Armand, bring any girlish flutters to her heart.

Though she viewed the play from the most privileged box-seat position in the house, she actually took in no more of the drama than had she been placed behind one of the massive pillars that supported the high, domed roof of her father's monument to the classical arts.

She had so meant to enjoy the play, too. But it had been a long and trying day and her personal problems had been brought to a harrowing head. She had been forced to make a momentous decision.

Beside her, Colby Vane wriggled like a small boy in church made testy by the complexities of a sermon he couldn't comprehend. He rustled his crib under her nose.

"Yuh know, this hyar play don't make the doggonedest scrap o' sense t' me," he whispered.

"Shh!" she replied quickly.

Colby scowled. "Don't know that it makes much diff'rence if anyone overhears me anyways."

"People are trying to *listen*."

"Aw, crap! No one c'n unnerstan' thet Frenchie lingo."

"Well, I don't want to talk," Lorena said curtly, straightening her slender shoulders.

"Can't see the hell why not. Damn sight more sensible than sittin' hyar like a row o' stuffed dummies . . . Hey! Did yuh see what thet French woman did t' the actor feller jest then?"

Gulliver Vane's voice came from behind them, seeming to boom in Lorena's ear. "Settle down, son!"

Lorena coloured and cringed. Thank God she would have to endure these foolish hicks not one day longer! Her

159

mind was made up and her plans were laid.

Tomorrow she would leave Argos City for good. It was no use trying any longer to convince her father how abhorrent she found his intentions for her future. She would never succeed, even were she to tell him how Colby had mistreated her that afternoon at the Arnott place.

At best, her misguided parent would accuse her of having invited trouble. At worst, he would tell her there was nothing to it, that she should manoeuvre her offender into an early marriage in order to accommodate his healthy lusts.

No, she had to escape the trap before it was well and truly sprung.

"Father," Lorena said quietly, turning to Bennett Maxwell. I have the most dreadful headache. Do you think we could step outside for some air?"

Maxwell frowned. "Surely you can wait, gal. It's just about the end of the first act . . . We'll take a stroll soon as the curtain comes down. That's any moment now, I reckon."

Lorena breathed her relief. It was then, from somewhere back of the auditorium, in the vicinity of the lobby and box-office, that the first gunshots rang out.

★ ★ ★

Some moments earlier, Marie Guisard consulted a gold timepiece crafted in Geneva by Baume & Mercier. It was a token of appreciation, *naturellement*, from Mademoiselle Gisèle. Life in the shadow of a famous celebrity had its material rewards. Also, Madame Guisard saw places and met people she would not have otherwise.

She shook her grey head sadly. The people and places were not always as uncouth as this Wild West, and she had ventured into the palaces of princes and dukes . . .

But she must not think about that now. It was a consolation that at least the dangerous gunman Monsieur Dillard had departed this regrettable scene.

Madame Guisard smiled to herself.

And above all — *toujours* — was the immense satisfaction of knowing that the world's leading tragedienne relied on her as a companion and secretary. No, more — as she would on a mother. To have Gisèle's trust was worth more than a thousand gold watches.

The time! Any moment now the curtain would be falling on the first act of *La Dame aux Camélias* and she must be in the small room behind the opera house box-office to collect the takings.

The terms for the American tour were generous. Without expenses. Gisèle's ensemble collected the equivalent in gold coins of five thousand francs per performance, plus half any takings in excess of fifteen thousand francs. And tonight they were again playing to a full house. So there would be heaps of gold for faithful old Marie to pack into the well-used Louis Vuitton bag!

She stumped along to the office on her heavy feet. The cultured young New Yorker Edward Carter and a man she had not met before, but whom she took to be a clerk, were waiting for her.

"Ah, Madame Guisard! Ever punctual. I must say. Indeed, a little early," said Carter. He looked professional and efficient himself in long-tailed coat and striped trousers. *Un galant homme.*

The old widow wagged her head. "We must always follow Mademoiselle Bourdette's instructions. *Exactement.*"

Carter laughed at her seriousness. "You're a good trouper, madame. Come, here is the gold, all neatly counted out into hundreds in these little canvas sacks. I've checked them myself. Perhaps I can assist you put them in your bag, then I'll walk with you back to the railroad cars."

"You are very kind, Monsieur Carter." She allowed him to fill the scuffed chamois leather bag, which he also helped her hold open. When they were finished and ready to leave, Carter opened the door for her.

"After you, Madame Guisard . . ."

She felt pleased and comfortable, but as she stepped out into the theatre lobby, a voice said from beside her, "A minute, *señora*!"

The ease vanished from her mind and the smile from her face. The mustachioed Mexican who stepped forward from where he'd clearly been lurking beside the door was big — huge-bellied and with bulbous eyes that shone with malice. She felt her stomach turn over.

She had heard all about the American frontier's outlaws and *bandidos*, and white or Mex she had not the least desire to confront one.

"What is it?"

"You will give me the bag. It is much too heavy for an old woman, es *verdad*!"

She trembled, clutched the precious

164

property more tightly, and took a step back.

Edward Carter jostled in front of her. "What the hell is the mean — ?"

The Mexican had drawn a revolver, which he spun, bringing the barrel into his hand. He swung it, and the butt caught Carter flush on the temple, felling him instantly. He laughed contemptuously; Madame Guisard screamed in horror.

Thought of death for herself did not frighten her. But that good people should be hurt, maybe killed, and her mistress' earnings robbed made her heartsick. "The bag, *señora!*"

Behind her the clerk made a scramble and she heard the scrape of an opening drawer.

"*Gringo* dog!" the bandit spat, his leathery brown face twisted with fury. This time he fired his gun, deafening Madame Guisard to her own scream.

The clerk went flying back across the small room, crashing into chairs and cabinets. The desk drawer he'd snatched out fell with a clatter. Its smaller contents spilled and rolled. A pistol he'd never gotten his hand on landed with a thud. The clerk's back came up against the wall and he slid down it, crumpling with one rattling cry.

Then a volley of shots shattered the sudden, deathly hush that followed the echoes of the first. It came away from the box-office, from across the lobby by the opera house's imposing front entrance.

"Mil diablos!" the bandit roared.

But as Madame Guisard swung her head at this new shock, he grabbed the bag and shoved her off balance. Long past the age for being nimble on her feet, she went sprawling heavily to the floor.

11

Playhouse Mayhem

ALONG about the same time that he drained his stock of beer, Joshua Dillard recognized that he was having second thoughts about his professed indifference to what was going on at Bennett Maxwell's opera house.

Changed your ideas some, haven't you, he asked himself.

Some, he agreed silently.

Mixed together, Gisèle Bourdette and her dumb Hercules, Henri Rabier-Roget. were too much for him to swallow. Purely poison.

But the business of the guns beset him like a persistent blowfly that kept on circling his head and settling on him however many times he tried to brush it off.

The setup smelled.

He puzzled over it again. The coincidence of the two jamming guns might mean anything or nothing, but if *all* the guns handed out to the men of the Bourdette company were useless, he would know some deep game was being played.

Such a caper would have a purpose. Maybe it would be an innocent, well-meaning one — like greenhorn actors' protection from their own lack of gun savvy.

But it could also be that someone had set their sights on Gisèle Bourdette's gold.

The first thing would be to step along to the opera house and check out some more of the guns. If he found them amiss, then he'd have more than idle suspicions, and maybe — just maybe — he'd condescend to go back to Edward Carter and talk turkey.

He rolled off the lumpy truckle bed and onto his feet. He tugged on his boots, using the leather straps sewn into the fourteen-inch tops, all the while justifying to himself what he was planning on doing.

"Can't just go traipsing off outa the country leaving these folks to get theirselves murdered by some bunch of blackguards," he murmured. "Besides, word might get around I left 'em in the lurch."

He hitched on his gunbelt.

Joshua left Ma Hoadley's boarding house, his urgent footsteps crunching the gravel of the short walk to the front gate, which he neglected to re-latch. He damned his restless hide to perdition, but at the same time part of him secretly rejoiced at the return to unfinished business.

With the performance under way, the crowd had filtered inside the opera house long since and its precincts looked pretty much deserted.

But Joshua's pale gaze narrowed at the two Mexicans loitering in front of the high, open doors between the massive sandstone pillars. These two hardcases were no theatre patrons, nor even ushers. They were *pistoleros*, if he'd ever seen any of the type.

He strode on toward them purposefully. One of the men stepped into his path, spitting from his mouth the end of a limp brown-paper cigarette.

"Sorry, *amigo*, but you cannot go eento the opera house."

"Why the hell not?"

The man shrugged insolently. "The show eet ees started."

"So . . . what's that to you, feller?"

"I have orders." The Mex hissed his words. "I geeve you good advice, *amigo*."

Joshua glared straight back. "That's twice you've called me *amigo*. I reckon you should know I'm kind of particular who calls me friend."

The Mex gunnie's complexion darkened. But just as things were looking dangerous. Joshua became aware of raised voices in the lobby. Before he could figure the significance of this, a gun was fired.

Instantly, he grabbed for his own hardware, and so did the pair barring his way.

Joshua fired. *Boom! boom!*

The Mex spokesman stumbled and went to his knees, a dark stain spreading on his shirt just below the shoulder.

His *compadre* hurled his lithe body to one side, his sixgun darting into his hand, a roar of Spanish profanity on his lips. The gun bucked and blasted as his finger gave a reflexive tug on the trigger.

The Mexican's swift dive had saved him from Joshua's second shot, but his own slug was aimed only in Joshua's general direction and though it plucked at Joshua's sleeve, it buried itself high and uselessly in the towering masonry of the opera house frontage.

Nor did he get to fire a second.

Joshua calmly put his third bullet through the muscle of the *bandido's* upper thigh, and he writhed futilely and painfully where he had landed, rolling, in the dust.

Other men were coming running, but caution hauled them up short of the scene of the gunfight.

"Self defence!" Joshua rapped.

He stormed on in into the opera house, smoking iron in fist, guessing now that he was messing with a hold-up and that he'd disposed of two lookouts.

Edward Carter was sprawled dead or senseless in the doorway of the box-office. Marie Guisard was a whimpering heap of sealskin ulster not three paces away from him.

Backing away from them, swinging the bulging leather bag Joshua had first seen in Gisèle's hands, was a third Mexican whom Joshua later was to learn was the locally notorious bandit chief 'Loco Louey' Velarde.

And he, too, had a gun in his paw. Joshua ducked below the stone surround of the ornamental pool and fountain that formed the classical centrepiece of the lobby not a milli-second too soon.

Velarde fired, and the bullet chipped fragments off the cold breast of the inanimate nymph who poured water from a never-empty shell into the pool around her feet.

The ricochet whined out through the main entrance into the darkness.

"Hell's bells!" Joshua had come close to getting himself killed in his haste. He should've known better. "Bastard good as had me cold."

He made no attempt to return the fire. The reason was simple. He couldn't afford to go off half-cocked. There were only two bullets left in the cylinder of his Peacemaker, since he always kept the hammer resting on an empty chamber.

"I'll wait till I've got him dead to rights."

His assailant realized the jig was up and he could make no exit via the main doors. He retreated down a passage that ran to one side of the closed doors of the auditorium.

Joshua edged after him.

Velarde snarled. "*Vamos, gringo* fool, or I will kill you!"

The corridor ended in a secured door marked 'Private'. Joshua thought he had his man bottled up. But even as he levelled his gun, Velarde fired again, and in the moment Joshua pulled back, he turned and smashed the lock with one mighty kick of his solid boot.

The door gave onto the wings, a cluttered backstage area and the actors' dressing-rooms. As Joshua took up the chase again, he saw astonished stage crew and actors gaping in the amber half-light at the rude invasion of their workspace.

An actress screamed when she saw Velarde's gun.

Joshua crouched low and felt the angry, fanning whistle of a bullet go over his head. Miraculously, he went unhit.

Velarde apparently figured too many bodies stood between him and escape this side of the stage. Nor did he relish charging across the open stage; maybe his pride forbade it. So he took to a narrow spiral staircase made of iron that led to a gallery in the space above and behind the proscenium.

Was this the panic of a trapped rat, or the cunning of a jackal? Joshua wondered.

One of the French actors produced a revolver, but when he apparently went to shoot at Velarde, Joshua observed with part of his brain that nothing happened.

Joshua boldly climbed the stairs after his quarry. Through the arch of the proscenium, he briefly glimpsed the seated rows of spectators, faces white blobs in the gloom, rising in tiers and surrounded by a gilded crescent of boxes.

Up above, aside from Velarde, Joshua could see only one solitary flyman among the ropes and weights and pulleys, like a sailor in the rigging of a ship. Here, he could dare return Velarde's fire without fear of hitting an innocent bystander.

He smiled inwardly. "It's him or me." He surely had the stickup artist cornered now. Everything hung on who would loose the first accurate bullet.

Velarde was in shadow, passing between two curving, iron-hooped structures under the roof rafters. But the instant Joshua saw him pause to turn and fire again, he sent flame and smoke lancing from the Peacemaker, expending both his remaining shots.

He cursed as neither found its mark, and the Mexican cried out in triumph at what he clearly saw as the easy target climbing up below him, picked out by the glow from the line of flames that was the footlights at the front of the stage.

A whining shot creased Joshua's left shoulder, gouging skin and flesh. He knew the next one, the last, would finish him. and he anticipated the heavy impact of the slug tearing into his body or his skull . . . how it would throw him off the stairs into the blackness of oblivion.

It never happened.

After a sudden whoosh, like water from a pump, a yowl of shock rent the drifting powdersmoke. Joshua heard a clatter as Velarde let go his gun and it bounced off the iron plate of the walkway and went tumbling to the stage below.

Joshua looked up to see water splashing everywhere. The shadowy structures Velarde had been passing between were huge vats suspended under the roof for instant use in case of fire — which Joshua recollected was a regular cause of unscheduled tragedy in the theatres of the day.

One of Joshua's bullets had holed a vat and the jet of water that sprang from the leak had hit Velarde, either knocking his six-shooter from his fist or shocking him into dropping it.

Joshua flexed his shoulder. He concluded no bone was broken, despite the burning sensation and the sticky dampness of blood. It was plenty sore, but he wasn't about to bleed to death.

Ignoring the wound as best he could, he holstered his gun and pounded up the rest of the stairs.

With a rumble of pulleys the curtain was being lowered on the stage, but Joshua could still hear the buzz of excitement and perplexity that gripped the audience.

He closed in on the infuriated Mex. "You're finished! Put down that bag, *bastardo*!"

"Fat chance!" Velarde jeered. He swung the bag at the crazy *gringo*.

Joshua warded off the blow, sickeningly aware of the dizzying drop to the boards of the stage below and the precariously narrow width of the iron walk and the frailness of its safety rails.

"Damn you!"

Joshua's hands tightened into fists. Favouring his numbed left, he put his head down and rained powerful blows to the disarmed bandit's body.

The wind was pummelled from the gross belly. Gasping for air, Velarde released the bag, which immediately went over the edge of the iron deck, plummeting to the boards below.

But Velarde still had tricks to pull.

For a man of his bulk he was swift and agile. With a foul oath, he stooped and snatched out a wicked boot knife. He let his arm carry on, swinging back to its fullest extent, giving it the momentum to return in a murderously forceful upthrust. If he'd made contact, Joshua's belly would have been ripped open and his guts spilled.

Joshua was no stranger to dirty fighting, however. He'd started back-stepping the moment Velarde's hand had reached to his boot. As the knife came up, he aimed a kick at it.

Thunk!

The driving toecap split Velarde's knuckles and the knife went the way of the gun and the bag.

"*Santos*! I will tear you apart with my bare hands!"

But Velarde was deprived of the chance to make good his threat. For

Joshua, in kicking the knife out of play, lost his footing on the slithery wet iron.

All at once he crashed against the spindly handrail which instantly bent to the impact of his full weight. When it could give no further, it parted at two joints. Joshua pitched backwards off the gallery.

Velarde gloated. "Break your neck, stupid Yankee!"

Joshua smashed onto the top edge of a flat made of coarse, painted paper over flour-sacking and lumber framing. It buckled up, split clear from top to bottom, and Joshua, his fall partly broken, cracked his head on the hard floorboards with sufficient force to knock him out without fulfilling Velarde's fiendish exhortation.

His senseless body rolled limply, brought up like a tossed rag-doll against a canvas backdrop.

★ ★ ★

Luis Velarde saw the people below rushing to cluster round the inert form of his unexpected foe. If he was not mistaken, this was none other than the cursed ex-Pinkerton, Joshua Dillard, whom he'd been told was out of the picture.

The fat was in the fire.

Overall, things had gone very wrong, but he'd observed with satisfaction that the French actors had no functioning hand-guns with which to impede his flight. That much at least had run according to plan.

Like as not, Dillard was dead or dying this time, too.

To his chagrin, Velarde had lost the snatched bag of gold. Even now the babbling foreigners were reclaiming it. His efforts hadn't brought him a *centavo*. But he could get out of this fix with his skin intact. And there would be another chance to help himself to the theatre company's riches . . . *Mañana*. Tonight, Lady Luck was frowning on him, not so? His lost wager at the cockfight proved that.

Velarde slunk quickly to the dark end of the gallery where he reached out and unhooked a loop of rope attached to a pulley. He let the loose end fall to the far-side wings of the stage and lowered himself down, hand over hairy hand.

Only the solitary flyman, who'd watched everything shivering with fear on his high perch, saw him go and when he yelled out a late warning to his colleagues below they were making too much noise of their own to hear him. A coming young actress who didn't know when to stop rôle-playing was busy having hysterics.

In the confusion, Velarde scrambled past dressing-rooms to a stage door and got clean away to hit the dust for his refuge in the hills.

12

Tip-off?

GISÈLE BOURDETTE had not known such violent excitement since the siege of Paris, when with loyal Madame Marie Guisard and a few friends she had patriotically run a military hospital in the cavernous basement of a Left Bank theatre. This was not exactly hostilities on the scale of the Prussian bombardment. Gunfire, after all, was different from shellfire, though one could be as deadly as the other. But the attempted robbery had all the elements of sensation and the potential for publicity that she loved.

Edward Carter and her Marie had been injured and an innocent clerk shot dead. Oh, what horror! But two real, honest-to-badness *bandidos* from across the line had died also, and the gold had been saved by the valiant Mr Dillard.

Even now Joshua, still unconscious, was being carried at her orders to the Palace railroad car. A doctor she'd summoned and paid for out of the takings had given permission — indeed, urged — that he should be moved to the most comfortable resting-place available.

The patient was badly concussed and bruised, and it was a miracle he didn't have a skull fracture, but as far as the medico could ascertain, none of his bones were broken. The blood in a bullet crease high on his left arm had coagulated and was scabbing even before it could be cleaned and dressed.

Gisèle could not be done with the subsequent acts of *La Dame* fast enough. After reassurances had been delivered to the audience and the curtain went up on the second act after a slightly extended interval, she resorted to the technique called *déblayage*. She delivered the lines in a racing, sing-song manner, relying on the natural melody in her golden voice, scarcely bothering with meaning and totally ignoring nuance. She even missed out lines.

How much would these non-French cow-tenders and their sun-shrivelled women understand anyway? She simply caressed them with sound. Monotonous, some might say. But there would be others to argue strongly that it was unspeakably sweet and penetrating.

In the farther reaches of the Americas, the spectacle she presented was surely reward enough for the audience: her own beauty; the wonderful wardrobe of imported costumes, delicately transported everywhere her company went in thirty-nine trunks.

At last the performance was over. Gisèle limited the curtain calls to a mere nine. Henri Rabier-Roget complained bitterly. Lack of talent somehow gave him a keener than average appreciation of applause.

"What does this ill-mannered haste serve us, mademoiselle?"

Gisèle simply ignored his question and left him behind her among the rest of the cast on the curtained stage. He sniffed petulantly.

She guessed he would console himself with morphine. As yet, the habit had few physical manifestations — mainly just the needle marks which in their clinches on stage and elsewhere she could see like mosquito bites along the veins of his arms. But she knew from experience that as the habit deepened into addiction, Henri would lose his one asset, his magnificent physique. and degenerate into a hollow-cheeked, twitching bag of bones.

Then, Henri would be of no use to her. Nor, perhaps, would he have any use for her. What she had seen of morphine victims, they had no appetite for anything — work, love, even food — nothing except their morphine.

These were unlovely thoughts. Gisèle became all the more determined to restore the strong and competent Joshua Dillard to her entourage for the duration of her American tour at least.

For a woman of her background, changing out of stage costume and dressing was a lightning-fast operation. Escaping attention before it could develop, she hurried back to the railroad depot with only a hard-breathing Madame Guisard in her wake.

The old retainer gulped in the ripe air that drifted from the empty cattle pens and loading yard.

"Faugh! This place will be the death of me yet," she said. "And what, my dear Gisèle, are we to do with the brave American lying in your car?"

Gisèle had a ready answer. "You will leave him to me, Marie. You have suffered cruelly tonight and must take yourself instantly to your quarters. Here, let me take the money bag."

She used a tone of voice that made it clear to Madame Guisard that she was to be left to her own private devices.

Knowing of old that argument would be futile, the faithful servant bade her goodnight. Her mistress was forever and always the subject of her own unbridled passions as was a spoiled and tyrannical child.

Gisèle went directly to her Palace car bedroom and lit the lamps. It was both an excitement and a disappointment to see the American adventurer deposited on her bed, minus his boots, but fully clothed and seemingly asleep.

She sighed, remembering how it had been for them that first time such an incredibly few hours earlier. The blood tingled in her veins.

Soldier of fortune? Shootist? Plain saddle tramp? Whatever they called him, she knew that restored to waking life and fitness he could take care of her in all the ways she wanted.

Meanwhile, she would watch over him . . .

But sitting something out was never

Gisèle's style. Only minutes later, she impatiently drew closer and reached out a light, slightly trembling hand.

★ ★ ★

Joshua Dillard came round the first time in darkness and silence. He knew immediately that he'd been moved and his creased shoulder had been bandaged. He sniffed at the air, noting a stimulating perfume that was both exotic yet recently familiar.

His body ached and his head swam as he lifted to peer at the black shapes that bulked densely elsewhere in the closed warmth of the room.

He groaned and decided not to pursue inquiry. "Aw . . . don't make no nevermind!"

It was sufficient for now to know he was alive and had more than mush between his ears.

He slept, and the next time he woke was something else. Light, deft fingers were undoing his shirt buttons and loosening his clothing. Even through his closed eyelids the light was uncomfortably bright. He went to move, but the busy hands pressed down on his hot bare chest too firmly for him to resist. And maybe their cool touch was soothing and welcome, too.

"Dahrrling, is that not more comfortable for you?" said a voice that could only be Gisèle Bourdette's. And he knew where he was.

She leaned over him, blocking the light. He flicked open his eyes. The delicate skin of her face was flushed over the high cheekbones, and the pupils of her slightly slanting hazel eyes were dilated. Her tongue peeped redly between coral lips.

It defied common sense and decency, yet even in his groggy state Joshua could not avoid a physical reaction to her closeness.

"Yeah," he breathed huskily. "I guess it is more comfortable."

She trailed her fingernails down his chest and stomach to his navel, her eyes falling ahead of them.

"No," she said. "I think not. It is very tight for you here." She put her hand on the visible swelling at his pants front.

"Ignore it. I'm too tired to keep it in check."

"I must release you." The practised fingers, swift and light as a pickpocket's, undid more buttons. There was nothing of the feather touch, however, about the way they tugged aside the wings of constricting fabric, and closed around the leaping hardness of him and fondled and caressed.

"Do you know what you're doing to an injured man?"

She smiled down at him. Her free hand was already busy at the side of her dress, loosening her own fastenings. "But certainly. I will bring you healing and a deeper rest."

"I don't know I've the strength for a dose of your physic," he murmured with little conviction.

She let go of him and put a finger on his lips. "Hush and lie still, ingrate! I owe you much and it will be a pleasure for me to do all the work."

The dress fell abruptly to Gisèle's ankles. He saw that she wore no underthings. He swallowed, watching her fluid movements, the free and immodest exposure of her naked female parts.

Joshua was a man of the nineteenth-century West and, despite what had already passed between them, woman as an aggressor was something of a shock to him, though it was not the shock of disapproval.

She stepped with supple ease out of the ruffled ring of silk and straddled him on the bed, smooth knees alongside his taut midriff.

She leaned forward so the firmness of an erect nipple brushed his lips tantalizingly before she eased back till her buttocks were pushing against his penis insistently. She raised herself, letting his straining tip trail down to find her woman-scented oiliness, then she forcefully descended, impaling herself.

She gave a moan of delight. Arching her spine and throwing back her head, she worked herself up and down, her slim hips heaving and swivelling astride him, pushing him ever deeper inside her with each plunging descent.

Joshua's whole frame jerked rigid time and again as he boiled over clamped in the saddle of her loins and the breath whooshed from his lungs. He felt his powerful climactic spurts rapidly expending his capacity to match the demands of her urgent passion, but her cries became ecstatic.

"*Mais oui*, Joshua! *Encore*! *Encore*!"

She reached behind her and between his legs and he felt her cupping his testicles, and nestling them up against the wetness as though she longed to attach them to herself, if not absorb his genitalia totally.

With failing vigour, he thrust upwards

and one last surge pumped unexpectedly through him.

"Oh yes, that's it!" she sobbed with pleasure.

He was drained, but her manipulation and flaring excitement kept him big and it seemed many more gasping minutes before she finally became limp herself with the languor of fulfilment and lowered her trembling, panting torso onto his chest.

Joshua, too, was short of breath. He was also long on wonder. This had been a coupling outside any in his experience. But then a famous French actress was a sight different from any woman he'd ever lain with before, and he doubted whether there was any other quite like Gisèle Bourdette anyway.

Should he have resisted her? He pondered the question but came up with no good reason why he should have.

She'd ridden him madly like a bronco-buster, and he conjectured whether the sensations he was feeling might be akin to those of a woman taken by force.

Or maybe, he thought ruefully, of a cow who'd been thoroughly milked.

He was still smiling at this bizarre analogy when they drifted, satiated, into sleep.

★ ★ ★

But Joshua Dillard did not find the peace Gisèle Bourdette had promised him. The actress was surprised and chagrined to find that though their fornication had left the Western gun-man spent physically, his mind was still active and troubled.

He tossed restlessly, pushing out of her embrace and rumpling the bed covers. When she touched his brow, she found it was hot.

Did he have a fever?

He began to mumble in his incomplete prostration.

Words emerged from the gibberish.

"Too sharp for greasers . . . a tip-off . . . inside knowledge . . . "

What did these strange American phrases mean? Gisèle could not fathom their apparent import, although her command of the language was extensive enough for most purposes. Eventually, she divined Joshua was referring to the attempted robbery at the playhouse without knowing why — unless it was for the mention of 'greasers' which she'd gathered during her travels was a colloquialism for Mexicans.

But Joshua had successfully thwarted the brigands, hadn't he? That was why she'd given herself to him — as reward, she rationalized.

She placed a cool hand on his forehead again, and he seemed to calm. "It is over now," she whispered. "The gold is safe. You are safe. We are safe."

The reassurances, or maybe just the comfort of her voice, seemed to have the desired effect. He sighed gustily and turned onto his side.

But a while before dawn, when grey light was starting to seep in around the roller blinds, embellished flamboyantly with her own coat of arms and motto, Joshua succumbed to a fresh fit of raving.

He sat bolt upright. She would have sworn from the blankness in his eyes that he didn't even see her, though the cover she'd pulled over them was tossed aside, exposing her to the waist.

The rush of cool air brought out little bumps all over her creamy breasts and her nipples began to swell. But Joshua was blind to her involuntary charms and the seduction of the warm bed. She was peculiarly bereft by his inattention.

"What's wrong?"

"The guns were fixed," he said. "I must know who fixed the guns."

He rolled off the bed to his feet, tugged up his pants and began buttoning. Once he was roughly dressed, he strode to the door.

"This caper ain't finished yet. I'll not

be back till I've gotten to the bottom of it."

Her skin crawled the more. She felt rejection and something besides, and it was not a good feeling.

13

Big Man's Orders

THE gunsmith's establishment was on Main Street, four doors past the Paradise Saloon. A crude sign, misspelt on a bleached board with a running iron, said: Emerson Petrie, Guns Sold & Repared.

Joshua Dillard hammered on the locked door with a clenched fist. He drew only the attention of the old roustabout in the high-crowned hat who'd spoken to him on his arrival in Argos City. Joe had been sleeping in another doorway across the street, but came hobbling over, ripping a fresh chaw off a strip of tobacco with his stained and broken teeth.

"Howdy, Mr Dillard. What's bitin' yuh this time?"

"When does this goddamn gunsmith

open up?" Joshua said. He was unthinkingly curt.

"Ain't no call to get a shuck in your snoot," the oldster said. "If'n it's urgent an' yuh like, I'll go knock 'im up at his residence."

"He knows you?" Joshua's doubt moderated his tone.

Emerson an' me are ol' pards, but he got the breaks I didn't, I guess. Him runnin' the only gunshop in town, the money jest nat'rally fell his way.

Joshua groped in his pocket and jingled coins. "Fetch him, and I'll stand you a bottle of the good stuff."

He paced the boardwalk out front of the shop another couple of dozen turns, then Petrie showed with Joe the loafer at his elbow.

The gunsmith was a small ancient with an uncombed shock of hair and stubble on his cheeks. The face hair was reddish, but time and harsh light had bleached the hair on his head to white and straw. He had a permanent squint. Since his trade would call for close work, it evidently didn't interfere over-much with his eyesight.

He nodded a greeting and put a key in the stout lock of his shop door. "Heerd 'bout what yuh did last night at the opry house, Mister Dillard. Reckon thar ain't nobody in Argos City thet ain't. What kin I do fer yuh?"

Before answering, Joshua tossed Joe his reward. "Don't drink it all at once." He turned to Petrie. "A word in private. And maybe a look at some of your stock."

The pair went into the shop and Petrie closed the door behind them.

The place was an Aladdin's cave of firearms. Rifles and handguns of every age and type cluttered racks and benches, from the old Kentucky to the latest Winchester repeater, and the earliest Walker to the newest Colt. Remington, Sharps, Henry, Savage, Merwin & Hulbert . . . their products were all on display here, whole or in pieces — gleaming new or corroded with age and ill-use — along with equipment Joshua couldn't put a name to.

A strong reek of gun oil caught in his throat. "It's about the guns you supplied at Mr Maxwell's expense for the Bourdette theatre company."

Petrie turned away and reached for a long, oil-smudged and gunpowder-grimed apron hanging from a hook. Joshua thought he detected a nervousness in the gunsmith's manner that he was using the movement to mask.

"Oh, yeah . . . a big order fer revolvers of all types."

Joshua picked up a Colt six-shooter from a scarred bench where it sat alongside an empty vice. He thumbed open the loading gate and rotated the cylinder. It span smoothly. He pushed the gate back into place.

"Functions well enough," he mused, as though to himself.

"Shore, Mr Dillard. Second-hand. Reconstructed. I do good work hyar. Did yuh wanna buy it?" Petrie popped a pair of rimless eye-glasses on his nose and peered at him.

Joshua looked around the shop before replying with his own question. "I reckon you must know your business and all, so what kind of roguery was it that every damn one of them revolvers for the Frenchies had a broken firing pin, a jammed cylinder or somesuch?"

Petrie rested shaking hands on the shop counter. "I dunno thet I should say."

"If you don't tell me, you'll have to answer to the regular law — a court mebbe," Joshua bluffed, putting iron in his voice.

Petrie thought it over. He rasped a hand over his chin. "Orders, Mr Dillard," he said in a tad higher than a whisper. "Secret orders. I knowed it weren't right an' there'd be questions asked, but it would of cost me my business not to toe the line . . . Shore — all them guns was duds!"

"Why, man?"

"Cos Bennett Maxwell insisted it was done thet way. Don't ast me why — ast him! But don't tell the ornery devil I put yuh onto it. Maxwell's the boss man in this town. If'n yuh mean to make a livin', it don't pay to buck Big Ben!"

Joshua figured he'd found out as much here as he could. "It's high time someone was bringing things to a head with Mr Bennett Maxwell," he said.

He dropped the renovated Colt back on the bench and barged on out the door. "Thanks, Mr Petrie," he flung back.

He didn't see the gunsmith smile thinly; didn't hear him mutter, "Brace Big Ben an' yuh'll be lettin' yuhself in fer real trouble, mister."

★ ★ ★

Lorena Maxwell was at home alone in the Maxwell town house with only a disinterested Negro housemaid to take care of her needs. The woman, she suspected, regarded her, like so many other Argos City folk, as standoffish. She left her strictly by herself unless summoned.

Well, that was jim-dandy by Lorena. Nothing now stood between her and her plans. Soon she'd be shaking the dust of this country off her heels. It had very little to offer her.

Colby Vane hadn't been the first cowboy to try to court her, but he surely was the most dangerous because he had her father's blessing. The rest of the pests and clodhoppers had soon realized it was useless to sweetheart her. Usually, they didn't stay clabber-mouthed about it either. Many the time she'd overheard some rejected hopeful dismissively 'vow and declare' she nothing but a 'smooth hide' or a 'scantling'.

They'd say, too, 'she can't count ties' but that was not true, because Lorena was range-bred and knew pretty well how to repair a barbed-wire fence and everything. It was a case of she didn't want to.

But it was all over now. A small carpet-bag was packed with the barest necessities and she'd be slipping out just as soon as she'd finished her early breakfast.

She picked at a boiled egg, trying to decide at exactly what point she should instruct the Negro maid to go deliver her farewell note to Colby Vane. She was proud of its triumphant wording, informing him she would not be keeping their luncheon date that day, or on any other for a long, long time . . . if ever.

Images of Edward Carter imposed themselves everywhere in her thoughts. She had a feeling he liked her, but he was too absorbed in smoothing the path for Gisèle Bourdette for any girl to take his fancy. What she planned would force him to take notice, and the very least she was banking on was his sympathy and co-operation. She dared to assume he would allow her them.

She dimly heard commotion at the

front door. An early tradesman who would get short shrift from Polly, she concluded distractedly. But the kitchen entrance was at the back, and before she'd worked out she was mistaken, she was confronted by the gunfighter Mr Joshua Dillard.

The Negro maid wrung her hands behind him, framed in the abruptly open doorway. "He shoved past me, Miss Lorena! He surely do have no manners!"

Lorena jumped to her feet and took a step back from the table. She felt ridiculously guilty, like she'd been caught out in something underhand, but she quickly recognized this was the product of all that was occupying her own mind. And as God was her witness, she really planned to do nothing terribly wrong, nothing to interest an ex-Pinkerton detective.

"Mr Dillard!" she said, collecting her wits. "Do you intend making a habit of rude entries into our dining-room?"

The man was shameless. "Where's your father?" he snapped without preliminary.

"He isn't here!"

"I see that. Where has he gotten to?"

"To — to the ranch, I expect. He left last night, straight after the play. He was very upset."

Joshua Dillard seemed to sneer. "I bet he was. And what's the matter with you? You look like you were seeing a ghost."

"N-nothing." But that was a lie. She knew something was wrong, though as yet she couldn't guess what. "Why do you want to see my father?" she asked bravely.

"Him and me are going to have a palaver. About guns. Dud guns. I want to know what his game is." He nodded and turned. "I'll be right off on the road to the B-Bar-M, Miss Maxwell. Your pa had better be there."

Something cold clutched at Lorena's heart. Dud guns . . . what was Dillard taking on about? But her father was strong enough and powerful enough to look after his own interests. This did not affect her.

Did it?

★ ★ ★

Henri Rabier-Roget had fallen into the company of strangers.

After the tramp-like *agent* Joshua Dillard had been whisked back into the Bourdette fold and the performance at the opera house completed, the actor had taken himself off to nurse his grievances alone at the Paradise Saloon. His fellow thespians seldom sought his company — plainly the result of their jealousy, of course, he told himself. But as leading man, and Gisèle's chosen one, it was his right to enjoy special privileges.

At the saloon, in a backyard privy, Rabier-Roget alleviated his disgust at his lady's present behaviour by shooting more morphine into his veins.

His confidence boosted, he told himself he had only to wait. Dillard might yet die of undiagnosed injuries. If not, Gisèle would eventually tire of the lout; perhaps he of her — he was clearly the drifting kind.

But meanwhile supplies of his customary solace were dwindling. The morphine gave him a feeling of extraordinary well-being and vigour, but latterly he'd been requiring larger doses to gain the effect.

"I hate it, I love it," he confessed his ambivalence to the neatly dressed Mexican who, for reasons he failed to conjecture at, befriended him in a shadowed corner of the saloon. "But chiefly I love it. It is sublime."

"*Si, señor.* I understand," his new-found friend said. "You must have more. It can be arranged."

"It can?"

"Of course. We have hidden fields in the mountains where opium poppies are grown, and secret factories where the opium is digested in limed water and the morphine recovered. You are very lucky, *señor*, for I can let you have a little . . . "

His last shot had boosted some cockiness back into Rabier-Roget. "A little, *mon ami*? I am riding the rails and need a whole stock."

The Mex's eyes gleamed in the gloom. "I have good friends who can take you to the *jefe* who controls all these matters — a general *muy magnifico*."

Rabier-Roget frowned. "It will cost a lot of money."

The Mexican shrugged. "Maybe . . . maybe not. There could be services you can render my principal, *amigo*. I do not know, but I have the feeling."

Rabier-Roget frowned some more. "I have no time. Unless I quit my position, I must leave on the special train tomorrow."

"The moon is full and the *jefe's* camp is not so far. The business can be done tonight."

So Rabier-Roget rode out of Argos City with the pusher's *compañeros* and met Loco Louey Velarde at his *posada* off the high back trails.

The Frenchman was flattered by the attention given him by the commanding, rather dandified Mexican leader. Though he realized he was being drawn out, he was not averse to spilling his troubles. You didn't make bones about such things when you craved morphine.

Velarde took it all in, plucking the end of a black moustachio and narrowing his bulbous eyes.

"I am a valiant fighter for my people and the betterment of the masses," he finally informed Rabier-Roget, puffing out his chest. "I want to help you, but the *dinero* you have is not enough. I need plenty *dinero* to further the cause."

Rabier-Roget's fuddled brain tried to take the self-proclaimed rebel's point. Was this Mexican chief trying to tell him no in some roundabout way? He felt disheartened.

"This is what I told your friend in the town. He spoke of services I could render you, but I knew it was foolishness."

"Let us say he played the hunch, and he could well be right."

"How is that?"

Velarde smiled and spoke very slowly.

"Your Madame Bourdette and her agents will be carrying much *dinero* out of Argos City tomorrow. The *norteamericanos* have not treated you well, especially Joshua Dillard. I spit upon that one. May the devil fly away with him!"

"You have understood my trials perfectly, general. What you say is the gospel fact."

"Together, then, we might teach them and your unappreciative compatriots a little lesson. At the same time I will take some of their gold in consideration of my — er — assistance to you, and to aid the poor who are under my protection. Not so?"

"It sounds an excellent idea, general,"

Rabier-Roget said, getting the drift and bobbing his head. "Give me the morphine I desire and I will help you play whatever tricks you like, to punish them. They deserve no less."

Velarde patted his shoulder, chuckling craftily. "Not so fast, *amigo*. We will give you one half the morphine you desire. The other you will have after the business is done. Now listen very well . . . "

14

The Rancher's Secret

JOSHUA DILLARD left the Maxwell town house, departed the residential quarter and strode purposefully through the dusty streets toward the livery barn where he'd stabled the trusty black. The hitch racks along the way were deserted and the boardwalks empty. But above the falsefronts on the east side of the street the sky was a flaming pink.

He walked in through the stable's broad double doors. The rows of stalls to either side were about half-occupied and the place was filled with the mingled odours of fresh droppings, hay and leather. He took a lungful and bellowed for attention.

The night hostler appeared at the door of the office, rubbing bleary eyes and tucking the tail of his shirt into his pants.

"What's the rush, friend? Last I heerd, yuh was open to offers fer the black."

"Change of plan. Several changes," Joshua said, tugging a rolled and greasy greenback from his pants pocket. "This'll cover expenses for now and I'll be back later to settle up."

He went back to the black's stall, took down the blanket and saddle draped on a rack by it and threw them across the glossy back. He cinched down the saddle quickly, put on the bridle, raised boot to stirrup, swung up and headed out.

Soon he was burning the wind on the road south from town. His long-term plans were no more clear-cut than they ever were. By the time he could get back to Argos City, he guessed the Bourdette Special would have steamed out. Possibly he'd rejoin it someplace down the line, but like as not he wouldn't. It wouldn't be the first time he'd lost money on a job that had soured. But he felt that rancher Maxwell had suckered him personally over the guns, and here and now he meant to have a reckoning.

Joshua was not familiar with the terrain, but the points of the compass were impressed on his mind like a sixth sense, born of a lifetime of wilderness riding, and this was not entirely open prairie. It was largely a matter of picking the right forks in the trail.

He was still a half-dozen miles from where he reckoned the B-Bar-M home-lot would be when he entered Maxwell's vast holdings. Bunches of the cattle baron's branded herds dotted the range every which way. Once he had to pull out of a draw to dodge a bunch that crashed, tongues lolling, out of the brush that clothed its slopes. No one was driving the critters and Joshua saw no ready explanation for their behaviour.

The sun was lifting into the brassy mid-morning sky when the headquarters of the empire — the B-Bar-M ranch-house and its long, low outbuildings and corrals — hove into view. Evidently, Big Ben had built with a view to permanence and defence in troubled times. The 'big' house had walls of adobe that looked fully two feet thick and a parapet ran round the flat roof behind which riflemen could have crouched.

Joshua gigged the black into a trot. A trio of punchers were standing outside the bunkhouse door when he rode into the yard.

"That's him!" a whisper travelled clearly. "Joshua Dillard, the gunfighter that put paid to the opry house robbery."

Joshua put a hand to the rim of his hat. "Morning, gents. Is the boss around?"

One of the punchers cleared his throat. "Guess it ain't our business to stop yuh moseyin' on up to the house, hombre. But the boss, he's sorer 'n a boiled owl today. Don't tell us we didn't warn yuh!"

"What's eating him?"

The spokesman shrugged. "Ain't no way o' knowin' sich things. Sensible folks jest hev their time cut out keepin' their own noses clean."

Off to the house, Joshua heard a window creak open. "What do yuh want, gunslick?"

Bennett Maxwell was glaring down at him, his face reddened with what might have been anger. Plainly he was not disposed to lay out a welcome mat.

"A word, is all. In private, unless you're apt to talk turkey in front of your crew."

"None o' the lip, Dillard!" Grudgingly, he added, "Walk on up."

Maxwell met Joshua at the door and showed him into a room equipped as an office. Joshua dropped his trail-dusty hat onto the top of the big black desk.

"I came about the guns you got Emerson Petrie to fix."

"Ain't none o' your business, mister," Maxwell said flatly.

"I aim to persuade you otherwise, Mr Maxwell, and I can't see no sense in your being evasive."

"By hell, yuh might of loosened Petrie's mouth, but yuh don't scare me, Dillard!"

"I saved your guests' money last night. Things could've unfolded mighty different. I reckon I deserve some explanation."

Jaws clenched, Maxwell appeared to give this his consideration. "Yeah, I'll give yuh one. It don't bother me none." His eyes glittered shrewdly. "I figured them French fops couldn't be trusted with real guns that could fire an' kill. Why, yuh could of bin deader 'n a doornail yuhself if'n they had."

He settled back in a swivel chair and smiled triumphantly. But Joshua didn't share his satisfaction.

"You're a damned liar, Maxwell. I can tell there's more to it than that."

Maxwell leaped up and hammered

his fist on the desktop, making papers and Joshua's hat jump. "Sonofabitch! No man tells me I'm a liar in my own house. Git out, mister, or I'll have yuh thrown out!"

Joshua said heavily, "I ain't no small-town peace officer you can twist around your finger, Mr Maxwell. I want you to know right now that I'm taking this — "

He was stopped dead in his tracks as a young man pounded into the yard outside like his pants were on fire. He was astride a hard-ridden, sweat-lathered roan and spilled himself off it at a dust-smothering run. He was yelling fit to bust his lungs.

"Mr Maxwell, sir! Mr Maxwell! It's Lorena! Yuh gotta stop her! The gal's plumb crazy! Yuh can't let her quit!"

"Colby!" Maxwell jerked. "What the hell? *Lorena quittin'*? Quittin' where? Is the kid gone soft-brained?"

Maxwell shouldered past Joshua as though he wasn't there. He stormed down a passage and out onto the stoop to meet the lunatic rider. Joshua traipsed after him, wondering.

The boy called Colby pulled a crumpled sheet of pink notepaper out of his pants pocket and flashed it under Maxwell's nose. Joshua, at the rancher's elbow, caught a whiff of the perfumed paper.

"See? She must of lit a shuck with them goddamned Frenchie actors and their New York minders! I found out she was seen at the railroad depot. She's stowed away on the blasted train, I tell yuh!"

Maxwell took the note and pulled it flat to read it. Joshua strained to catch a glimpse of the written words, noticing that Maxwell's jowls were quivering as he read. There was a semi-apologetic line or two about a broken luncheon date, then the thrust was much as the boy called Colby had said, except Lorena didn't mention just how she was leaving Argos City or with whom.

Joshua saw Maxwell make a big effort to collect himself. He looked over at the gaping punchers outside the bunkhouse, then back again to Colby Vane.

"Take Hollister and the boys, Colby," he snapped, gesturing to the hands. "Ride to the junction and try to stop that train!"

Colby shook his head. "We'll never make it, Mr Maxwell!"

"God a'mighty, boy!" Maxwell roared. "We gotta do somethin'! Just try, will yuh?"

Colby shuffled and backed off, then he turned and ran back toward his horse, still blowing from the run.

The three punchers were headed for a corral where a string of cow ponies grazed. Hollister yelled, "Leave your blown hoss here, Colby! Take a fresh 'un."

The four spurred out of the B-Bar-M home-lot in a cloud of dust.

"I could use a stiff drink," Maxwell said. He shambled back to the house. Joshua was surprised at the sudden transformation in him. The man had gone into some kind of shock. Why?

Joshua went after him. "It ain't as though your daughter's dead," he said.

Chinking decanter against glass, Maxwell tossed down a liberal dose of spirits, but didn't move to offer Joshua any. He laughed hollowly. "She might just as well be!"

"I don't savvy."

Maxwell shot him a hunted look, then averted his watering eyes. "Yuh don't know the half of it, Mr Clever Dick!" But his bombast had lost its fire.

"Tell me your story, Mr Maxwell. What's the panic? What's at bottom of all this?"

Maxwell dropped the whiskey glass and spread his hands in a loose gesture. His face was white. "That Mex bastard Loco Louey is gonna wreck the Bourdette Special an' loot it, is what!"

Joshua was staggered. "How do you know?"

"The dirty son's bin blackmailin' me

years. He's gotten a spy on my payroll, in the cookhouse. The miserable critter limped in with word no more'n an hour back that this was his plan . . . an I was to sit tight an' let it happen, seem's how my help had only loused up previous arrangements for him to get his thievin' hands on the theatre take."

"Well, I'll be damned!" Joshua said. "Blackmail . . . I'm beginning to understand why you didn't want me around and supplied the dud guns." His tone was accusing and contemptuous.

Maxwell flushed. "Awright, so I tried to foul things up for yuh. So what? Come right down to it, what choice did I have? Fact is, I'd gotten into deep financial trouble. My herds had bin infected with Texas fever. The northern markets wouldn't accept them. All my spare fat had bin gobbled up buildin' that there opera house. I faced ruin an' couldn't meet Velarde's blackmail demands no more.

"The skunk had already bled me white when he got me to line up Gisèle Bourdette's *dinero* for him. Since I couldn't give him the stuff, we agreed he could take hers instead!"

Maxwell had himself another drink. This time he didn't bother with the tumbler but put the decanter straight to his lips and gulped. When he lowered it, he visibly swayed.

Joshua shook his head musingly. "Some blackmail hold this Mex *bandido* must have over you," he said by way of a prompt.

"The worst!" Maxwell said, looking at him with a partly vacant expression, as though he was talking just to himself. "It's my daughter, my Lorena . . . Louey controls the Border whorehouses an' he found out from her blood mother she's half-Mex! Yeah, my late wife never carried her. Her health was too frail. She was consumptive, an' fool that I was I found compensation in the arms of an upstairs girl in a *cantina* across the line."

Joshua waited.

"The *puta* got pregnant," Maxwell said, "but she didn't want no truck with no part-*gringo* child. So when it was borned, I brought the babe home an told my childless wife it was an orphan. We brought Lorena up as our own daughter. With my wife dyin', Lorena an everyone else has bin kept unaware of the deception."

Joshua knew he was still missing the vital point that left the rancher devastated. He groped. "But what happens if you tell Velarde to go take a jump and he makes these things known?"

Maxwell drew himself up with the half-drunken dignity of a small-town big-shot — and Joshua cottoned the muddled morality that held him in Velarde's power.

"If my daughter's origins are made known, sir, I'll be dishonoured an' Lorena will be made an outcast. Fer certain sure, Colby Vane, the son of the president of our stock association, won't lower hisself to bed the half-breed daughter of a damned greaser whore!"

"The hell with cow-country prejudice!" Joshua said, bemused by Maxwell's priorities. "A trainload of innocent parties are maybe riding to their deaths. They include your daughter — and as I figure it, it won't much matter whoever and whatever her mother was when the train gets wrecked and the lead starts flying!"

Maxwell weighed his blunt talk owlishly. Joshua wondered, too, whether unburdening himself of what he thought was the cause of his oppression had brought him to a saner appreciation of the real fate that could be hanging over his cherished offspring.

"Shit!" Maxwell said. He crossed the room suddenly, yanked open a closet door and hauled out a twin-holstered gun rig. He started buckling it on. "Let's shake some more facts outa that gimpy cookhouse Mex. We gotta get after Colby an' the boys. They're

228

gonna need all the help they c'n git
— but fast!"

★ ★ ★

Lorena didn't dilly-dally after Joshua
Dillard left. She kept her head and
put swift, finishing touches to a big
spray of freshly cut flowers, despite her
fingers seeming to be all thumbs. She
attached a piece of pasteboard, neatly
inscribed in copper-plate handwriting:

*"Farewell to Mademoiselle Gisèle
Bourdette from Bennett Maxwell and
the management committee of the
Argos City Opera House. A parting
token of our appreciation."*

She bolstered her determination to
run away and justified herself by
reminding herself of her autocratic
father's intentions for her future; the
flesh-creeping touch of the repulsive
Colby Vane! For a girl to have to
submit to such things was stupid and
rotten wrong.

Eventually, she would have to throw

229

herself at the competent Mr Edward Carter's mercy. But somehow she felt the sophisticated New Yorker was a man of a different stamp to any she'd met before. She didn't think he would force her to return to her misguided father's heavy rule.

Armed with the flowers and her bag, Lorena went directly to the railroad depot and bluffed her way aboard the Palace car itself without challenge. In the event, the flowers served mostly to boost her own confidence. It was just on sunrise and those folks on the move had their own business to go about.

She checked furtively that Gisèle's panelled and carpeted travelling parlour was empty and slipped in. A single lamp with a trimmed wick guttered as she quickly closed the door and put down the flowers on a Turkish ottoman.

Should she hide right here? It seemed as good a place as any with its rich jumble of plush furnishings. Being slim, she was able to make herself relatively comfortable in the small corner space behind the upright piano.

She was still there, feeling a little stiff and cramped, when presently a steam whistle shrilled its warning note, a bell clanged and the train lumbered into a rattling crawl out of Argos City.

Lorena's great adventure had begun! And even she didn't suspect how close she was to more excitement than she'd ever bargained for . . .

15

'Judge Colt'

"THIS the hombre?" asked Joshua, stabbing a thumb at the crippled Mex sluicing pots behind the cookhouse.

"That's him," said Bennett Maxwell.

Joshua cold-eyed the *peon*. "You're going to sing, friend. You're going to tell us everything you know about Loco Louey's scheme to wreck the train!" His implacability struck perceptible fear into the Mexican. "Velarde weell keell me, *señor*, and rueen Meester Maxwell," he whined, his face glistening.

"That don't cut no ice anymore!" Joshua said, and pulled out his Peacemaker. He thumbed back the hammer and the cylinder clicked menacingly. "Talk fast, or you'll be nursing a second game leg!"

232

"Madre de Dios!" Velarde's pawn dropped pot and scraper and gabbled all he knew. A section of the railroad track had been pulled out on the steep grade that led up from a canyon to a place in the mountains called Tomahawk Pass. When the locomotive was derailed, Gisèle Bourdette's rear car would be uncoupled by someone aboard. The car would roll back into the canyon, where the waiting bandits would rob it.

"Eet ees possible some passengers weell be abducted and held for ransom . . . "

Horrified, Maxwell looked at his watch. "Enough jabber! Less'n Colby caught up with the train at the junction, we gotta ride!"

Joshua was aware of that. The chances the train had been stopped and delayed, and Lorena removed, were desperately slim. Time was running out to thwart Loco Louey and his gang of desperadoes. A surely bloody showdown loomed.

Maxwell rapidly fired a Winchester three times in the air for help. It rustled up a posse of merely three range riders working close to the house.

This scratch crew was the best that could be mustered. "The numbers ain't going to be on our side," Joshua reflected to himself gravely, "but Maxwell and his outfit have got to fight it out. They don't have the option to involve the regular law. The verdict will be Judge Colt's. No trial, no jury, no nothing."

They set off at a hard gallop. Pell-mell, they streaked across a wide section of prairie, tore through clawing brush and splashed across a creek. Surmounting a grassy knoll, they spied Colby Vane and his party riding back toward the B-Bar-M.

Maxwell raced out hell-for-leather to meet them and confirm they'd failed to beat the train to the junction. "We was pushing our luck," Colby Vane said. Maxwell gave orders pronto for them to join the mission to Tomahawk Pass.

"We'll whip the bastards yet!" the rancher swore. "We can still cut across the broken country an' get to the pass ahead of the train."

With four extra bodies, Joshua figured their chances against a fired-up band of Mexican hardcases as being a mite better — maybe close to even numerically — yet far from good.

* * *

"*Alors, ma petite*, you have chosen a headstrong way to show your devotion to the arts!"

Lorena gulped. "I would be greatly honoured, Mademoiselle Bourdette, if you would let me travel with you. I am sure Mr Carter could think of some small way in which I could repay your kindness."

The gently swaying train was labouring up a steep grade and steam billowed whitely past the windows. Gisèle looked up at the curved, scroll-worked ceiling of her Palace car in a musing manner.

"Ah, yes, Edward . . . he has spoken of the charming Miss Maxwell, that I know."

"He has?" Ridiculously, Lorena's heart leaped.

"But of course. Edward is an American gentleman who wishes to be honourable in everything. Between you and me and the bedpost — that is how you put it? — he found you adorable . . . Alas, while it is one of the things he 'must say', he must also deny it to himself, because he has always to move on, committed to his business. So the Anglo-Saxon honour cheats a man of amorous disposition."

Lorena felt her cheeks warming. Having a deeper complexion than the French actress, and indeed most Argos City girls of her acquaintance, she hoped it didn't show. "Oh, I'm sure you must be mistaken," she flustered.

Gisèle shrugged and smiled. "I am charmed by your naïvety, Miss Maxwell."

236

She might have gone on to say more about this fascinating state of affairs, except that the toiling train abruptly lurched to a juddering halt, almost pitching her off the *chaise longue.*

"Grand Dieu! The train has hit something!"

"Perhaps the loco has jumped the rails!"

A hissing of steam in the sudden stillness tended to corroborate Lorena's guess. But more distantly, she heard the puzzling crack and counter crack of what sounded to her ears like an exchange of gunfire. Together, the pair rushed to the door at the front end of the car.

Gisèle thrust open the door, then stopped short as she stepped out onto the small railed platform. "Henri!" she exclaimed. "What are you doing?"

Lorena took in the astonishing scene in one long, roving glance, partly through the opened door and partly through the windows to either side of it.

Up ahead, the locomotive had plunged to one side of the ascending cutting that carried its tracks. Steam escaped from its ruptured boiler. Train crew seemed to be scuttling in all directions around it, shouting orders and warnings.

On the rear platform of the next car, Lorena recognized the imposing figure of the theatre company's leading actor. But Henri Rabier-Roget didn't look so handsome now. His face was twisted in a maniacal grimace as he levered at the coupling between the two cars with a steel bar.

"Stop him!" Lorena cried. "If he undoes that, we'll roll plumb back into the canyon. We could be killed!"

★ ★ ★

Joshua hauled up his small force as it approached the railroad-slashed draw that led into the canyon below Tomahawk Pass. The need for breakneck riding across wild, boulder-strewn terrain was over now. The call was for stealth and subterfuge. He pointed to fresh sign of riders.

"Up ahead Loco Louey and his *compadres* will be waiting in ambush for the runaway Palace car, I guess. We're gonna ambush the ambushers! There's nine of us to encircle them, but if they hear us coming, it could blow the whole damn thing."

"No two ways about it," Maxwell agreed. "We've gotta fix this gang wholesale an' permanent. Five hundred dollars to the man who kills Velarde!" He turned to Joshua. "So what's your plan?"

"We leave the horses ground-tied here and sneak in on foot to fix the bandits' positions. When the train comes by, it'll be getting up steam for the pass and making a hell of a noise. The Mexes will be watching and hearing nothing else. That's when we make our play."

The nine slipped up the canyon from point to point, taking cover behind blasted boulders and scattered oaks, dwarfish and bedraggled where winds had whipped down from the pass twisting them into bizarre contortions.

A horse whickered ahead, and Joshua knew it wasn't one of their own.

The brigands were hunkered down, as he'd expected, near the foot of the incline. They'd bothered with no great attempt at concealment. The distinctive, high crown of a black sombrero, intricately patterned with gold braid, betrayed Loco Louey Velarde himself! He was to the forefront where a spur of jumbled rocks reached out near the tracks.

Joshua motioned his band to halt his own men, and counted all of Velarde's bunch he could see. A round dozen.

"Now we've got 'em!" he breathed, drawing his Colt. He waved his arm again in a circling gesture, and Maxwell's six punchers and Colby Vane spread out behind their quarries, pistols in fists. Maxwell himself drew up to Joshua's side behind a clump of prickly pear.

"Yuh've got 'em boxed in," he said. "They wanna argue, it'll be like shootin' fish in a barrel."

Joshua was cautious. "Touch and go," he said. "I'll offer them a chance, else it'll be a bloody business. We've got the drop, but there's more of them than us."

Only moments had passed when the distant rumble of the speeding train came to them on the wind and through their boot soles. The red locomotive exploded into sight, pounding the tracks, belching smoke and sparks as it built up power for the climb to the pass.

Below them, some of the crouching Mexicans raised a mocking cheer as the train clattered past. Under cover of the bedlam, Joshua and his company rushed forward to new points at the closest quarters.

Then, with the noise receding, Joshua rapped out a clear command. "Hoist 'em, greasers! Get those hands high! You're surrounded. Throw down your guns where you stand, or we'll riddle you! Hoist 'em!"

Only two of the startled Mexicans chose to obey the order and grab sky. The rest grabbed guns from cutaway holsters and answered with wildly aimed bullets. The fight was on.

Most of the B-Bar-M posse kept their heads down, forted up behind jagged granite outcroppings, picking the likeliest targets. The first man to fall was one of the surrendering bandits. He caught a slug in the back — part of the rain of indiscriminate fire from his *compañeros*. He writhed and screamed, agonized by the bullet that had torn into his intestines.

But Velarde's pack had the ferocity and daring of cornered rats.

Bullets whizzed over Joshua's head. Zinging ricochets sent rock splinters flying and blood almost immediately started to trickle from a cut where one jagged piece sliced his brow. A pall of grey powder-smoke drifted on the air.

Maxwell's cowpokes could choose to

return the fire — or crouch where they were and let the *pistoleros* turn the tide against them and force their way out of the cordon on relentless waves of gunfire.

To Joshua's left, a B-Bar-M man screeched. He'd poked his gun above a boulder and a *bandido* slug had instantly shattered his forearm.

Two of his pards shot back, and another Mex sprawled headlong, a raw, red hole between his eyes. "We got the varmint, Charley!"

The exultant cry was drowned in a fusillade. All hell broke loose. More casualties were sustained on both sides. The racket of gunfire and men's cries filled the canyon with ghastly echoes. Before long, Joshua lost track of how his side was placed. The Mexicans committed the folly of exposing themselves time and again, but they were the more experienced at gunfighting and ready to lay their lives on the line.

"It's their minds," Maxwell said.

"They don't think like us. They're fatalistic!"

"You haven't got a chance, Velarde!" Joshua bluffed. "Give yourself up before more men die!"

But Loco Louey was livid. Being caught with his pants down as he was about to stage his greatest coup was a savage blow to his pride. He snarled an oath as he recognized the voice of his tormentor.

"May the devils of hell take you, *Señor Bastardo* Dillard!"

He charged forward recklessly. Such a big-bellied man moving at haste cut an incongruous figure. But he flourished two pistols, both blazing, and that made him nothing for Joshua to grin about.

The gunman stood his ground, moving round to maintain cover, trying to aim his Colt. Everything, he knew, hinged on firing one effective shot as soon as he showed himself. He had no illusions. If he tilted the muzzle too high or jerked to one side and missed

Velarde's moving figure, he'd probably be dead before he could trigger again.

As he stalled, the unexpected happened. Bennett Maxwell surged to his feet, inveigled or panicked into rash action.

"Die, yuh scum!" he yelled, and fired the six-shooter in his right paw.

Joshua heard the ugly smack of the bullet striking flesh a split-second after the gun's report. He raised his head in time to see Loco Louey bare his teeth before he staggered and dropped his guns, putting his hand to a blood-spurting wound just beneath his throat.

The big Mex went down, flailing and coughing till a quick death glazed his muddy brown eyes.

Beside Joshua there was a second crash. Maxwell, too, had fallen to the ground, clutching his belly. "He got me . . . in the guts!" he gasped. "Hit bad. Guess I'm done for."

"You made a false move, Big Ben," Joshua said, quickly kneeling beside him. "Should of left him to me."

Maxwell looked up at him with a twisted grin. "I got the swine anyways. Lorena will be safe now. Keep my secret from her, Dillard. Colby will go ahead an' wed her an' the B-Bar-M will be saved by its merger with the Vane spread."

His voice faded to a whisper and he died with his eyes closed and a smile on his lips.

Joshua shook his head. "Man, you sure knew how to keep on being mistaken . . . right to the end."

He suddenly realized the shooting had stopped. He straightened up, breathing hard, wiping blood, sweat and hair out of his eyes.

Three members of Velarde's gang, demoralized by his killing, cowered before the B-Bar-M rannies, hands in the air. Another two had reached horses and were making a hurried getaway. The rest had been cut down in the gun battle.

"The train!" Joshua said. "What happened to the train?"

Colby Vane and two others were left in charge of the prisoners, and Joshua and the remaining fit punchers set off uphill toward the stalled cars at a brisk trot.

Thankfully, they found their assistance wasn't needed, other than for a man to ride to Argos City to alert the railroad company to the derailment.

Edward Carter had his arm around Lorena Maxwell, which confirmed Joshua's guesswork about where the rancher's daughter's affections truly lay. Knowing the grim news that had to be broken to her, he was glad Lorena had someone her shining eyes told him she was prepared to lean on.

Carter, too, looked as pleased as Punch. "I must say, if it wasn't for this plucky young lady and Mademoiselle Bourdette, it might have been very different. That despicable Rabier-Roget! They were forced to overpower him. It seems he was in cahoots with the gang that derailed the loco."

"Yeah," Joshua said. "We'd heard

about that. And I always knew M'sieur Henri wouldn't do to tie to."

★ ★ ★

Gisèle insisted on bathing and bandaging Joshua's cut forehead personally in the privacy of her Palace car bedroom.

"You must rejoin us for the rest of our American tour, *mon cher* Joshua."

Joshua grunted. With Rabier-Roget facing a probable court hearing and jail sentence, he could do a whole lot worse. Not that he cared for a surfeit of the kind of soft living Gisèle clearly had in mind for him. But for the time being . . .

Avoiding committing himself, he took up the small silver bowl from which the actress had washed his brow and studied the coat of arms and motto worked on its side. It was the same design that appeared on many other of the car's accoutrements.

"What's this?" he asked idly.

"It is my *devis*, my motto."

248

"Tant que je puis." he read. "What does that mean?"

"It means 'As much as I can'. And it is what I will do for you also," she said, an arch smile curving her dainty lips.

"Hmm," said Joshua. "I thought you already had, but I won't stop you proving me wrong."

THE END